I0618103

Beyond Reflection

Agio
PUBLISHING HOUSE

PUBLISHING HOUSE

698 Dogwood Crescent
Gabriola, BC Canada V0R 1X4

Edited by Michael Kenyan – michaelckenyon@gmail.com
Produced and published by Bruce Batchelor at Agio Publishing House
– bruce.batchelor@gmail.com
Cover design by Mikey Swallow of Little Blue Dog Designs –
info@littlebluedogdesigns.com – inspired by and using portions of the
painting by Deb Tivy that appears on the back cover
Group photo of the BWB members on page 203 by Maureen Richardson

Beyond Reflection
ISBN 978-1-990335-31-0 (pbk)
ISBN 978-1-990335-32-7 (ebook)

Agio Publishing House is a "greater purpose" company, measuring
success on a triple-bottom-line basis. We gratefully acknowledge that
we live, work and play on the unceded traditional territory of the
Snuneymuxw First Nation.

10 9 8 7 6 5 4 3 2 1ª

Beyond Reflection

A collaborative novel by the

BWB Book Club of Vancouver

Sue Johnson

Maureen Richardson

Linda Stevens

Deb Tivy

Joanne Webster

Cathy Kershaw

Judy Rothwell

Lynda Stevenson

Lea Tkatch

Eleanor Wright

Agio
PUBLISHING HOUSE

PART ONE

NEIGHBOURHOOD

CHAPTER 1

1987

A late summer sun was setting over Bowen Island. The day had been long and warm. The air was scented by the ocean breeze wafting up from Third Beach and in the distance an orchestra of seabirds was tuning up.

Jane sighed. Such a lovely evening. Shame to ruin it.

Jane and Julian were sitting on the outdoor patio at the Stanley Park Teahouse. He had used his connections to secure this particular table for its unimpeded view over English Bay, and now the waiter, dressed in a crisp black tuxedo, came to take their drink orders.

"Two dry vodka martinis, please. Hold the olives," Julian said.

"Very good, sir."

As the waiter turned away, Jane looked at Julian with surprise. "Martinis? You know I'm not a fan."

"It's time you became one, you're past thirty. In my family we always drink martinis on special occasions," he said. "And today is extra special."

She blinked into the setting sun, through the glare of the present, into the past. This wasn't the first time Julian had taken over a situation. It made her uncomfortable, but there was no point in making an issue of it. After all, this was going to be their last date.

This beautiful old building had been a military post in an earlier life, standing watch during the war for the safety of its nearby citizens, according to her dad, and now, retired from active duty, it was the Grand Dame of Stanley Park – a wonderfully romantic restaurant. It still stood silent watch, but over what? And why was she feeling on guard?

The waiter arrived with the drinks on a silver tray. She thanked him politely but Julian paid no heed. She felt him watching her. Then he reached across the table, pushed a long strand of dark hair behind her ear then stroked her cheek.

"You are absolutely lovely."

What was going on? He was not usually effusive. She leaned across the table and met his lips. The kiss was as gentle as the caress and she felt her defences being gently dismantled. His kiss always had that effect on her. She craved these moments as much as she dreaded them. How could she think straight when her brain was being highjacked by the sensory power of a grazed lip? Stay rational, keep a check on your emotions, girl – but here was this man, once again sending her reeling with the slightest touch.

They'd met the year before just around the corner at the Stanley Park tennis courts, each as a 'single' looking for a game. She had surveyed the empty spots on the court-side benches and selected one beside a man about her age. They chatted politely for a while and when a court became available, they rallied cautiously, each assessing the other's ability. Gradually, she had upped her game by adding depth and spin to her shots, delighted to receive the barrage of returns that forced her to reveal her A-level game. She enjoyed playing with men and was happiest when she didn't have to hold back.

Afterwards, they drank stale coffee from the kiosk and chatted about everything and nothing.

"So, what do you do?"

"I'm a reporter with CKVU."

She couldn't help but notice the way his thick hair swept gracefully across his forehead, softening the intensity of his intelligent grey eyes and square jaw. An unexpected smattering of freckles completed the wholesome boy-next-door look. "I guess your good looks are an asset," she said.

He laughed. "Actually, it's my voice skills honed on CKNW, 'all-news radio.' I've just moved on to TV reporting. I'm a backup anchor for the local news."

"How come I haven't seen you?"

"So far, I've only done a couple of broadcasts." He paused. "The early morning time slot," he added sheepishly.

They both laughed. After a slow walk back to their cars, it was clear they would become a couple.

Even as a young girl she had known what she wanted for her future – to work in health sciences – not as a doctor or nurse but doing research which could lead to treatments for the diseases that plagued humanity. Growing up in North Vancouver she had been one of the few girls from her graduating class to make the leap across Burrard Inlet to the University of British Columbia in Point Grey.

Microbiology was a field dominated by men but women were starting to push gender barriers aside and she was among the first through the gate. After completing her master's degree she started work as a researcher in the University Hospital Department of Hematology. Her natural intuitiveness and analytical mind propelled her to the position of assistant department head by her late twenties. She had been living in her Kitsilano view apartment for a few years, alone but dating when it suited her – carefree and in control – enjoying a life she had mapped out for herself when Julian Clements drop-shotted himself into her world.

Julian reached across the table again and took her hand. "This is our night."

They clinked glasses and she slowly brought the shallow vessel up to her lips and noticed something round and glinting in the drink – definitely not an olive! She plunged a finger into the glass and plucked out a glimmering diamond ring.

"I love you, Jane. You are the most extraordinary woman I have ever met." Julian got up from his chair and knelt beside her. "Will you, Jane Elizabeth Stewart, be my wife?"

"YIKES!" This was completely unexpected. How had she missed the cues? She had ruled out marriage long ago. No man could live up to her expectations. Marriage, while nice in principle, was simply out of the question. She stood and pulled Julian to his feet but before she knew it he had slipped the band onto her finger and delighted onlookers were clapping in approval. When she looked down their hands were clasped together, the ring glittering in the weak western sunlight. Oh my god! What just happened? He must think I said yes! Am I engaged to be married?

"Our lives together will be full of adventure," he said. "We will travel abroad and one day have a family, a boy and a girl and maybe a dog. It will be wonderful." He beamed.

She quickly replayed the last year in her mind. They had never talked about travelling, much less marriage or children. They had been focused on their work when not exploring physical delights. It had all been perfect as far as she was concerned, but now it was time to wind things up. Sure, he had introduced her to his parents, Bertrand and Sibyl, and had been a little impatient until she took him home for a Sunday dinner Chez Stewart – against her instincts: she did not take boyfriends to meet Bud and Doreen; didn't want them to get their hopes up that their strong-willed, independent daughter might be ready to settle down. But Julian had a way of pressing his agenda and she had gone along with it. Now this! What other clues has she missed?

Julian, clearly oblivious to her distress, was forging blindly ahead.

"I know you hate surprises but—" he paused for effect "—I have been offered a job as a correspondent with CBC television. Just think I'll be covering national and international news! I had the interview a few weeks ago and well... last Friday the offer came in."

She struggled to make sense of what he was saying. An interview... a new job?

"I remember thinking in March when Chernenko died and Gorbachev took over that there was going to be a monumental shift in world politics and I was right, look what is happening; this is a situation so unique that they had to invent a new word for it. Glasnost! Even as we speak Gorbachev is reaching out to Reagan and I think they will meet soon and it's possible I could be assigned to cover the story!" Julian's eyes were shining. He continued. "It will mean moving to Toronto, of course, and there will be times when I will have to go overseas but you may be able to join me. We'll have an exciting life, I promise."

She was still reeling from the shock of the marriage proposal, and now all this. Suddenly the vile cocktail in front of her seemed enormously appealing. She raised it to her lips and took a giant gulp. As the liquid scorched its way down her throat she scrambled to compose herself.

"But Julian, I'm in the middle of an important pharmaceutical trial... It could lead to major advancements in the treatment of leukaemia... and you know how personal that work is for me….” She was choosing her words carefully, trying to manage the anger surging inside her.

He checked himself. “I’m sorry I didn’t get to meet Clara.” And then he was off again. “Darling, after we move you’ll find another job. Hell, you won’t even need to work. We can join a tennis club and you can become one of those ‘ladies who lunch.’”

She reached for the martini again and hoisted it.

“Yah, and you could host cocktail parties and raise money for worthy causes,” he went on. “I can see you sautéing duck livers on Bunsen burners and passing around Petri dishes of crudités as you host biology-themed galas in support of lost kittens or something. Ya, and you could even wear your lab coat…

“Gotcha!” Julian laughed. “You should see the look on your face!” He bugged out his eyes in mock imitation.

Vodka spurted from her mouth and nose. She was laughing now too. The idea was beyond preposterous. God! He had a way of making her laugh no matter what the situation. When she was around him everything was lighter, funnier, more interesting. And he was the most thoughtful man she had ever dated. He had taken her to Bruce Springsteen’s *Born in the USA* concert at the Pacific Coliseum for her thirtieth birthday only a month after they started dating. He had gone out of his way to ask her friends what she would like and surprised her with the tickets. She hadn’t been happy about him approaching her friends without her knowledge but was able see that he meant well. After the Boss ripped through *I’m on Fire* and the Coliseum had gone wild, Julian had driven her home and walked her from his car to her apartment. On that cold, damp October evening she had started to shiver and he had guided her towards a towering pine tree, opened his overcoat and pulled her into his chest, closing the coat around the two of them.

The embrace and tender kiss they shared had stirred up feelings she had spent years repressing. In the weeks that followed, she'd tried to quash the intrusive thoughts that were popping into her head and distracting her multiple times a day. He was just another transitory boyfriend, after all. Men could be inspiring leaders, brilliant collaborators and good company on rainy evenings, but they didn't possess the qualities that would allow them into her inner world. Few women did either for that matter. Her mother, yes, and Clara had been allowed for many years, but to avoid unpleasantness she had determined that it was best to keep friends and lovers at a distance. QED.

Despite such intentions, keeping Julian at bay had been exhausting. And eventually impossible. It was the little things that had demolished what was left of her willpower; he was not bothered if she beat him at tennis, or at chess; he knew she liked her tea strong with milk and two teaspoons of sugar and that she loved white dahlias; he found her jokes funny. She had fallen in love. She had let her feelings cloud her judgment, and now look, things had gotten excruciatingly complicated. She had to end things before they went any further.

"What?" Julian looked confused. "This is a very big step for me, you can see that, right?"

"Of course… and I want that for you."

"Toronto is the centre of opportunity – for both of us," he said. "You will be able to get a better position there and you'll climb the ladder faster than you would here."

The waiter was standing by the table waiting to take their dinner orders. She asked for the Salmon Wellington and Julian ordered his usual, a 10 oz. porterhouse steak, medium rare, along with a bottle of Chateau Margaux. She would have preferred white wine with her salmon, but she knew how much Julian loved a dry red with his beef. Not a big deal. Bigger fish to fry, ha ha.

She concentrated hard on the pattern in the Irish Linen tablecloth, following the concentric circles in the white-on-white pattern with her index finger, getting to know them well.

"How could you not tell me you had applied for the position? How could you buy a ring and propose and then spring all this on me?"

Julian's face fell. He looked hurt for a second but regrouped quickly. "I thought it would all be a wonderful surprise; and that it would make you happy. Obviously I'm an idiot but you know how I get ahead of myself when I'm excited about something. And I've never been more excited in my life!"

"So I see. When does the new job start?"

"I haven't accepted the offer yet. I want you with me when I agree."

"When you agree?" she said coolly.

"I love you, Jane. I've wanted to marry you from the day we met. I want you by my side forever. You're brilliant, creative, and independent... so much like your mother."

She looked at him and smiled. "Thank you for saying that, it's a compliment to us both."

"I will be very proud to call Doreen and Bud my new parents."

She began working the ring from side to side on her finger. It was a perfect arc of white gold embedded with diamonds. No jutting solitaire to scratch a cheek, or worse, pierce a latex glove. It was astoundingly beautiful in its simplicity. She couldn't help but feel a sense of warmth and contentment as she thought about the love and companionship marriage would bring. She looked out the window at the sailboats gliding silently across the bay and the monolithic freighters anchored in the distance. She positioned the ring to capture the last of the fading sunlight but it was too late; the sun had dipped below the horizon.

She reflected upon how disappointed her parents would be. It was striking how well he had gotten on at the family dinner. He had listened to her older sister Helen's endless braggadocio about her children, talked football with Bud, helped with the dishes and even invited younger brother, Andy, to play rugby in the park with his old school chums the following weekend. By the end of the evening both of her parents had been smitten. Big mistake that introduction. And now what? She sighed, taking it all in – beautiful setting, beautiful ring, beautiful man.

She looked into Julian's hope-filled eyes. Impossibly irresistible. And yet again, she slipped. "I love you too," she said leaning in for a vodka-infused kiss.

By the time they returned to her apartment they were both giddy with anticipation. Jackets were dumped onto the floor and shoes flicked off as they made their way down the hall locked in a clumsy embrace. When they reached the bedroom she grabbed his shirt and yanked him inside.

❆ ✂ ❆

She awoke cloaked in darkness. With her bedroom window partly ajar she could hear the wind howling like a lost child. Her curtains swayed gently back and forth, letting in the yellow light of a streetlight. She heard the door click as Julian let himself out, headed off to his early morning assignment. She rolled into the middle of the bed, seeking out the comforting smell of his sweat and familiar cologne. They had made love ferociously, as if each was trying to devour the other. He was certainly her match in the libido department.

She rolled onto her back and stretched out her left arm. "Mrs. Julian Clements," she said softly. "Announcing Mr. and Mrs. Julian Clements.... Hello, my name's Jane Clements...."

As a child she had assumed she would eventually marry and have children. She would fall for an ambitious, caring man who would be a good provider and father. Most of her classmates had married years ago, some right out of high school, more after college. She had had multiple suitors along the way but had always ended things. Suitor, what a weird word. None of them suited. The dean of Applied Science held her interest the longest but he had dropped her after six months for a first-year home economics student. Of course. Her only regret was that he had ended the affair before she did.

She took a deep breath then let the air out slowly.

"Tomorrow I'll tell him."

She sat up in bed and grabbed hold of the ring. In one smooth motion she pulled it over her knuckle and off her finger. It was surprisingly easy to do, physically. She placed the ring on the bedside table and gazed at it bleary-eyed as a gust of wind flung aside her curtain allowing the streetlight's glow to fall onto it. Poor thing. It sat like a lone soldier, exposed, unprotected. Suddenly it released a tiny but remarkably brilliant flash of light. She blinked hard, trying to clear her vision. She stared at the ring, waiting, but the room remained dark.

She drew the blankets up around her but could not quiet the tremors that were overtaking her. Her mind was racing, pulling her from the comfort of her bedroom... dragging her away.... Sleep was out of the question, so she flung off the covers and swung her feet off the bed onto the floor. Donning the robe from the foot of the bed, she walked into the bathroom. As she stared into the mirror waiting for her eyes to adjust to the poor lighting, she was surprised not to see her own image in the glass. Instead, a pale-skinned girl with a round face and shoulder-length blonde hair gradually materialized. The girl was gazing at her sternly....

"Oh my goodness!"

Jane recoiled from the mirror and her hands flew to her mouth. Am I still drunk? But no, she felt fully in control. When she dared to look back, the image in the mirror was gone.

"Clara?"

She began pacing the short hallway between her bedroom and the other rooms of the apartment, her stomach clenched in a hard knot. "Breathe..." she whispered to herself. It was no use. Her brain continued churning, unearthing distant memories. "Breathe? That yoga stuff is obviously a load of crap," she muttered as she marched into the kitchen and poured herself a glass of wine from last night's half-empty bottle. She took the glass back to the bathroom, set it on the edge of the tub and turned on the tap. Dawn was still a long way off, she mused, as she lit a jasmine-scented candle and climbed into the tub. May as well get comfortable.

CHAPTER 2

1968

The excited chatter of dozens of tiny birds in the treetops outside her window tempted 12-year-old Jane from under the covers. She poked her foot out and, finding the temperature to her liking, not too chilly, she rolled over and opened her eyes. Her first glance, as always, was towards the low window that ran along the entire length of her bed. Tucked into a dormer in the attic, her bedroom was cramped but from her perch she could see over the front yard of her family's bungalow and across the roofs of the houses down the street, straight down to the dense forest that blanketed the foothills of Mount Seymour.

It was early April, Saturday morning, no grade eight classes to attend, no projects to work on and no adult-imposed obligations. The sun, swaddled in grey flannel clouds for months, had finally cast off its uniform. She blinked into the glare, letting the warmth caress her face. She sat up. It was a day not to be wasted by lingering in bed.

As she prepared to stand, the bedspread at her feet roiled and slowly Sophie emerged. The smoky, long-haired cat with her pop-bottle green eyes and flourish of bone-white whiskers was no longer Sophia Loren, her parents' favourite movie star, but old Sophie slinking from under the covers completely dishevelled. The fur on one side of her face was flattened while the fur on the rest of her head swirled and spiked in disarray. The end of the cat's tail, which had been broken, went off in a direction all its own, seemingly unconnected to the rest of her spine. Anyone who ventured to tickle her underbelly encountered mats of fur too numerous to count.

Sophie stretched, took stock of the situation, then set about the painstaking task of grooming – a futile activity that would occupy her entire day. Jane sat on the edge of the bed and gave the cat an affectionate roughing up which, despite her protests, she thoroughly enjoyed.

Jane slipped off her strawberry-patterned pyjamas and put on her favourite jeans. Before pulling a T-shirt over her head, she looked down at the soft swells forming on her chest wall. A problem. A few months ago when running down the school corridor she'd crashed, chest-first, through the exit doors, to be knocked breathless with pain. The pain had subsided but had not gone away entirely. The soft mounds confirmed her worst fears. Up until now she had been happy with school and home and friends and teachers and, well, life. What plans did her body have in store for her?

Her sister, Helen, had been a regular playmate until her bust developed. After that everything changed. With her mane of auburn curls Helen was considered by the relatives to be "the pretty one" but they quickly added that Jane was "the adventurous one" when they realized she was within earshot. This didn't bother Jane in the least since she valued risk-taking over appearances any day. A multitude of healing scrapes and minor scars on her forehead and knees were testament to how she hurtled though life. She loved the outdoors and spent many spare hours in the forest surrounding the newly-built neighbourhood on Vancouver's North Shore, happy to be in her own company. She had been identified a few years earlier as an advanced reader and accelerated a year in elementary school which had landed her in her current grade a year younger than her classmates. This had driven her even further inward.

She and Helen had shared a room for years and become very close despite the three-year age difference. They'd talked long into the night, Jane filled with wonder as Helen mapped out the newest neighbourhood mystery to be solved. Jane recalled the prickly mixture of fear and wonder that spread over her while listening to her sister's play scenarios. She would fall asleep dreaming of how they would unravel the mystery. The next Saturday they would play for hours, sometimes in their bedroom, but often in the empty lot beside them or in the forest, wherever the mystery took them. Sometimes they would give in to five-year-old Andy's pleas to join in, but only on the strict condition that he take on a non-essential role such as a small animal. Or if he was good, he could be a lookout. Andy always did as he was told, knowing that any infraction would mean the end of his involvement forever. Once, when the empty lot became the Sahara Desert, he was an iguana slowly flicking his tongue in and out of his mouth. At a pivotal moment he struck a majestic pose on a large bolder and stayed utterly still until a fly landed on his outstretched tongue. Without the slightest flinch he drew his tongue in, snapped his mouth shut and swallowed the fly.

That had impressed even Helen.

Those happy days were gone and all imaginative play had ended abruptly. Along with the arrival of Helen's new bustline she'd suddenly lost interest in what she called "childhood games" and now had little time for Jane at home or at school.

"All my friends have their own rooms," she'd whined one day about a year ago.

Their parents pointed out that the house was not big enough, this was not possible, but Helen could not be dissuaded.

"I'm too old to share with Jane. I need more privacy."

Jane had been crushed. She had no real friends other than Clara Sagan, who lived across the street. The Mason twins, Jim and Scott, lived three doors up the block but she rarely saw them outside of the schoolyard. They were a year older and didn't play with other children much except now and then in the summer when all the neighbourhood kids got together for a game of "scrub" or "cops and robbers."

The Stewart's cedar-clad bungalow consisted of a small living room, dining room and kitchen and three modest bedrooms, all on the same floor. Rather than moving, which their father had explained would be too expensive, it was decided that he would build a room in the attic for one of the girls. He toiled over the project for six months, working on weekends and in the evenings after finishing up at the police station. Even before it was completed, Helen had rejected the new room, complaining bitterly that it would be cramped and lack closet space. Worse, it was a flight of stairs away from the sole family bathroom.

And so the days of sisterly adventures were over and Jane was growing increasingly repulsed by Helen's emergent interests and new behaviours. While Bud crashed and hammered up in the attic and Doreen puttered in the kitchen, Helen lost interest in her grade ten classes and stopped doing any homework. She lied to their parents about how well she was doing until the quarterly report card arrived to set things straight. Subsequent evenings resulted in tears from Helen and tense discussions between Bud and Doreen. Jane wondered why

Helen thought it was worth it, but it was happening a lot, deceit followed by despair.

Equally incomprehensible, as far as Jane was concerned, was that Helen had become obsessed with fashion. Their shared closet was now stuffed with tight-fitting neon tops and short A-line dresses emblazoned with bold prints. Helen's old jeans were handed down to Jane and replaced with new ones with fitted waists and flared legs which widened from the knee down. This new wardrobe took centre stage and Jane's few things were crushed into an inaccessible corner. Even more irritating, her sister was occupying more than her fair share of the small space by spending almost all her free time in there, often with girlfriends, pouring over glossy teen magazines filled with pouty, emancipated models. And without asking, she had put up gaudy posters of rock-and-roll singers all over the walls. Peace and Love? Don't think so. Jane tried not to look at them but their eyes followed her round the room. It was as if they had moved in and she had become the outsider. There was no use in complaining to Helen and she knew it.

But worst of all, was that Helen's new ways of self-expression were not confined to the family home. She joined the school cheerleading squadron and obtained the pompoms and other paraphernalia that went along with that. While she looked attractive in her short, pleated skirt and crop top, she could not dance or keep time. She would throw her arms up when the others had theirs tucked into their waists and spin around as the other girls flopped into the splits. Jane found the spectacle of her older sister bouncing out of time and chanting tunelessly in front of the entire school acutely embarrassing. It was as if her sister had gone utterly mad.

By the time the attic bedroom was ready, Jane could not wait to move in. Back in January, she'd climbed the narrow stairs, pushed her bed tight up against the window and stuffed her clothes into the small dresser. After carefully unpacking her schoolbooks and notepads she'd flopped onto the bed and gazed up at the painted plywood ceiling with its simple glass light fixture. The room was perfect!

Today she tugged down her T-shirt and held up her tiny mirror to assess the unwelcome developments on her chest wall – twin betrayals by her own body. If Helen's transformation was any indication, nothing good lay ahead.

"Breakfast!" called Bud from downstairs.

She finished dressing and descended the steep stairs to the kitchen where the smell of bacon beckoned.

"Morning, Janie," said her dad as he turned over a pancake on the stove. "Ready for a daddy-cake?"

"Don't call me Janie," she said, marching into the room. "You know I hate it."

"As you wish, Lady Jane," he replied and made a slight bow.

She rolled her eyes and continued towards the red Formica table.

Undeterred, Bud pivoted and smacked her playfully on the bottom with the spatula. "Take that, your Haughtiness," he quipped.

"Stop it!" she cried. "Or Daddy is going to be doing laundry too!" With that she ran out of the room with him charging after her until he had her on the living room carpet, tickling her until she begged him to stop.

Bud returned to the kitchen while Jane stomped out the front door and sat on the stoop. Rosie loped over, wagging his tail and flopped at her feet. Burying her hands in his thick, sun-baked coat was like putting on mittens fresh from the dryer. The black Labrador cross had been adopted from the local dog pound when Helen was going through a "pink phase" several years ago. After insisting on gender-defying naming rights to the male dog, Helen had quickly lost interest in him. But to Jane, Rosie was the finest member of the Stewart family, consistently affectionate and approving, and she found herself seeking the comfort of his presence more and more often.

She went back inside once the rest of the family had gathered around the table. The kitchen was where they ate all their meals, save Christmas and Thanksgiving.

After breakfast Doreen picked up her purse from the counter. "Helen, Jane, dishes please. So, Bud, I am going to take the car now and do the groceries."

Bud frowned. "Taking the kids?" he ventured.

"Nope and if the shopping doesn't take too long, I'd like to get my hair done too," she said, snapping her purse closed.

"Doreen," said Bud, "I have to get to the hardware store at some point today. Tomorrow is Sunday – all the stores will be closed."

"And we need groceries," she repeated. "Listen, hon, I need to get off the side of this mountain every once in a while. It's driving me stir-crazy being here day in and day out. Maybe it's time we got another car."

The two girls eased out of their chairs and started to gather the breakfast dishes knowing full well where this was headed.

"Darn it, Doreen, we've been through this," Bud snapped. "I can't afford two cars on my salary. No cop can. Sure, the Sagans have two cars but he's in the car business and can get deals. What am I supposed to do? Work more overtime, so you can go to a goddamn hairdresser once a week? I already work bloody hard to support this family and what do I get? Constant pressure...."

"Stop it," said Doreen sharply. "Everyone knows how hard

you work. You don't have to make us feel guilty. I work hard here at home and I need a little time out of the house once in a while."

Bud stood up and strode into the living room, taking the newspaper with him. He plopped onto the sofa and shook open the paper, holding it up to his face. Jane and Helen exchanged glances as they stood at the sink. Doreen slid out of the kitchen, down the walk, got in the car and drove off. Only Andy remained at the table, worry etching his young face.

Doreen returned an hour later. Jane watched from the front window as Bud grabbed the keys from her in the driveway, climbed into the car and pulled out hastily leaving her standing there with two bags of groceries but no new hairdo.

The rest of this day would be best spent out of the house, Jane decided, so she pulled on her jacket, called for Rosie, and crossed the street to call on Clara. The two girls had been friends before but now that they were in grade eight together they were almost inseparable, working together on school projects, hanging out during breaks and on weekends.

They rode their bikes leisurely around the neighbourhood with the dog galumphing along behind them, pink tongue lolling out of his mouth. They visited the corner store and bought multicoloured jujubes, chewy caramels and bubble gum wrapped with tiny comics all with money Clara got from her mother. Back home they sat on the lawn in front of Clara's house and Clara snuck candy into Jane's pile and Jane slipped candy back into Clara's pile until they got into a full-scale tussle rolling around on the newly-mowed lawn.

"Say uncle!" Jane demanded, but Clara continued to struggle gleefully.

"CLARA!"

The two girls looked up and saw Mrs. Sagan standing in the doorway, arms crossed.

"Time to come in," she directed.

Clara stopped squirming and Jane let her up.

At the door Mrs. Sagan brushed the loose grass from Clara's clothing and the two disappeared inside. A moment later Mrs. Sagan stepped outside and clapped together the soles of Clara's shoes. Jane watched the grit and grass clippings rain down, then extracted her bike from the shallow ditch where she had parked it and wheeled it up her driveway into the carport. Her father was sitting on the front stoop, taking long drags on a cigarette. Rather than passing close by him, she entered the house through the carport door that led directly into the kitchen.

Doreen was chopping vegetables at the sink. "Have a nice time?" she asked.

"Uh huh."

In the hallway that led to the attic stairs Jane was accosted by Helen emerging from the bathroom holding both hands over her face. "Jane, tell me which side looks better." She uncovered one side of her face. She had applied turquoise eye shadow to the lid. Her lashes were thickened with mascara, and her eyebrow had been sculpted with the help of tweezers and a dark-brown pencil. The visible portions of her mouth were painted with raspberry coloured lipstick and her cheek was ablaze with blush.

Jane stared. Horrible.

"Now, look at this." Helen covered her face again then removed her hand from the other side, revealing a hint of taupe eye shadow, a thick swoosh of liquid eyeliner and spidery false eyelashes, top and bottom. Her lips were painted with a pale pink gloss and her cheeks were dusted with translucent powder. She moved her hands back and forth so that Jane could have a good look at each. Ghastly. Dreadful.

"Hum," said Jane. "Which looks better? Let's see… Bozo or Casper? It's a tough one."

Helen's hopeful expression changed to confusion then rage. She lunged but Jane was already scampering up the stairs to her attic sanctuary. The slamming of the bathroom door meant her sister had given up the chase.

Phew. Jane dropped onto her bed.

※ ✕ ※

That night, lying in bed after a silent supper, Jane listened to her parents talking in the kitchen. She could not hear their words but she could feel the tension behind the voices. She hated it when her parents were fighting. It was happening so often lately.

As usual, she lay on her side looking out over the galaxy of porch lights, the only illumination in the blacked-out neighbourhood. At the bottom of the street the shimmering ended abruptly and the dense darkness of the forest began. She lay in bed thinking about the animals that lived in the woods. There were many trails through the trees and people hiked there during the day. Chipmunks, squirrels, skunk and deer were often seen and on rare occasions someone would spot a black bear. And, of course, there was no end to the birds: robins, jays, wrens, crows, sparrows, swifts. She imagined the animals settling down for the night and her thoughts turned to her own life. Nothing was making sense. Her parents who used to be so sweet to each other were quarrelling. Helen, once so much fun, was now someone best avoided. Even her own body was no longer familiar. And what was going on with

Clara? Their games were taking on a much more physical nature.

Suddenly, a spark of bright white light caught her eye. It was fleeting, like a flashbulb going off in the distance, and she wondered if she had imagined it. Propping herself up on her elbow she watched intently, waiting for it to come again. But the night remained black above the forest and eventually sleep crept up and claimed her.

CHAPTER 3

Jane was jolted awake. Not fully aware of what was going on... too sleepy. But there it was again. She rolled over and looked towards the window. Suddenly the room was awash in light. Then she realized... lightning. She grabbed the bedcovers and pulled them over her head. But no thunder. In the middle of the night came the thunder. Now it was a real storm and rain lashed the attic window. The storm howled and swirled like angry spirits released by a witch's spell. All she cared about now was getting back to sleep. She stuffed her head under the pillow, holding it tightly against her ears and covering her eyes. She was warm, cocooned by the blankets. Sophie, as always, was cuddled next to her feet under the covers. She, too, was trying to ignore the storm.

What did the animals in the woods do during a storm? Did they have a dry place to wait out the weather? But worries about the badger, fox, mole began fading way and in a few minutes she was sleeping soundly.

❋ ✕ ❋

The next morning the front door slammed as Andy left the house but Jane lingered in bed until the smell of bacon and coffee wafted into her room. Her parents were preparing the usual Sunday fry-up, a treat made even more special because she knew it would be just the three of them. Helen stayed in bed past noon on weekends and there never seemed to be any disagreements between Bud and Doreen at the Sunday breakfast table.

They were not closely attached to any church. Bud's

parents, having emigrated from Scotland when he was four, had ties to the Anglican Church, but they were not strict observers. Doreen's parents referred to themselves as "lapsed Catholics." Out of an abundance of caution the young couple had decided that Sunday school at the neighbourhood United Church would be a good idea for their children. Helen and Jane refused to go after two sessions but Andy willingly got up every week and caught a ride with his buddy's family for the morning classes. He knew if he attended more than half the classes this year, he would get to go to church camp in the summer. And since his friends were all going, he wanted to go too.

"Good morning, Janie! Did you manage to sleep through the storm last night?" Her dad put a plate of crisp bacon in the centre of the kitchen table.

"Sophie and I both woke up… please, please—"

"I know, I know, don't call you Janie. I wondered if it would wake you, way up there in the attic. The lightning would hit you first!" He laughed.

"Bud!" said Doreen.

"I saw lightning right after I got into bed," she said.

"No, Janie – I mean Jane – you couldn't have, it didn't start until the middle of the night. I know because I had to get up at midnight and close the bathroom window when the rain started."

"Well, I saw the first flash much earlier," she said, sitting down and digging into the pile of bacon, buttered toast and fried eggs on her plate.

"Stubborn as a mule," said Bud.

"What are your plans for the day?" asked Doreen.

"I'm going to see if Clara wants to check the woods to see

how the animals fared. Maybe some small birds fell from their nests. Who knows what we'll discover."

Soon she was wheeling her bike out of the carport and down the street with Rosie prancing excitedly beside her. She knocked on the bright red door and Mrs. Sagan answered.

"Can Clara come for a bike ride?" she asked.

"I suppose. She's in the back yard helping her father wash the cars. Go around the side of the house," she directed, making it clear that Jane would not be coming through the house itself.

"No wrestling," she added as Jane parked her bike and ran to find her friend.

❈ ✄ ❈

Left alone in the kitchen to clean up after breakfast, Doreen and Bud worked in silence.

"Peace and quiet," he said.

"Nice try," replied Doreen. "I have something to say. I ran into Susan Miller at the grocery store yesterday and she told me she's started working part-time at the hospital. She was a nurse before she got married, you know, so she's gone back to that. Just a few hours a week but she really likes it. And... well... I've been thinking I'd like to try something like that too."

"That's ridiculous," snapped Bud. "What would you do? The last job you had was counter-girl at the dry cleaners and that was over fifteen years ago."

Doreen winced. "I know I didn't go to college but there are lots of things I can do."

"When would you have time? You have three kids to

look after, and the house. And why would you want to work anyway?"

"I could earn some extra money and help with family expenses. And I'd like to have a bit of money to spend on myself occasionally. And, well... I thought, maybe, if I earned enough, we could buy a second car." She lowered her eyes and waited.

✠ ✗ ✠

Meanwhile the two girls were peddling off together carefree and happy towards the woods with Rosie galloping alongside. They yelled "hello" to Scott Mason who was walking up the street towards his home. He smiled shyly and waved back.

It was rare to see Scott without his brother, Jim. There was only one other set of twins in their school, identical sisters who were always dressed alike by their mother. The girls had separate interests and rarely played together, but Scott and Jim, not identical, rarely did anything apart. And they did not seem to have any friends. Scott might be okay but he was so quiet. Jim, on the other hand, was unsettling. He was unpredictable. The kids in the neighbourhood were afraid of him. One evening last summer while all the kids were playing "kick the can" Jim, enjoying the game as much as everyone, suddenly charged out of his hiding place and viciously kicked the legs out from under a much smaller kid who was about to kick the can and win the game for his team. The poor kid went flying and ended up in tears. Jim claimed it was an accident but no one who saw it believed him. Most of the kids, including Jane, avoided him.

Jane and Clara rode into the forest on one of the well-worn paths.

"Are we coureurs des bois scouting new territory or trekkers lost in Patagonia?" Clara yelled.

"Not this time. We are searching for animals who might need help," Jane shouted back.

The woods were still damp, with branches and leaves dripping wet. Nothing appeared obviously ruined or out of place, but the girls continued splashing their way along the waterlogged paths, their eyes peeled for anything out of the ordinary. Clara took a spill off her bike and landed face-first in the mud. Jane skidded to a stop and laughed uncontrollably until a clump of mud hit her square in the chest.

"It's not funny!" said Clara. "My mom is going to kill me."

"There's no avoiding that now," said Jane as she snatched up a pinecone and bounced it off Clara's forehead. Soon they were pelting one another with musty-smelling clumps of soggy peat or whatever else they could get their hands on. The filthier they got the harder they laughed.

As the two girls walked their bikes up the road, tired and hungry but happy, Jane remembered what was awaiting Clara at home. She watched guiltily as her friend leaned her mud-splattered bike against the porch, opened the door of her house and stepped inside.

Entering her own house, Jane tiptoed across the hall and started up the stairs to the attic.

"Is that you, Jane?" Doreen called from the kitchen. "Can you come in here please? Oh my God. What have you been doing, rolling in the mud?"

"Clara and I were horsing around on the trails, that's all."

"That must have been some rodeo! Get yourself cleaned up and help me with dinner, will you? We need a salad."

As they worked together, they chatted amiably, but Jane could sense that her mother was distracted.

"Is everything okay with you and Dad?" she asked, not really wanting to hear the answer.

"It's fine. You don't need to worry about any of this. Your father is upset because I want to try something new. He only wants what's best for the family, of course. We both do. We are just seeing things a little differently at the moment," Doreen explained. "Other mothers are getting part-time jobs, that's all. It's becoming more common as children reach school age."

Jane didn't like the idea of her mom not always being at home. She imagined what it would be like to come back to a cold, empty house. It was understandable that her father might feel the same way but there seemed to be more to it than that.

After dinner the girls went to their rooms to do homework, while Andy took a bath. At 8 p.m. everyone gathered in the living room, Bud adjusted the rabbit ears, and Ed Sullivan materialized from the static on the TV screen. They marvelled together at the jugglers and acrobats and rolled their eyes at the crooners. For that hour every Sunday night, it felt as if none of them had a care in the world.

Come bedtime Jane ran upstairs. She couldn't wait to dig into her new Ursula Grimes mystery. She sat propped up on her bed with Sophie curled up beside her and lost herself in The Secret of Angus Downs as the stars came out. Then she saw it – out of the corner of her eye – a brilliant flicker of light. She propped herself up and leaned toward the window. Would it come again? A repeat of last night's wondrous thunder and lightning spectacle?

But no, the sky was clear; she saw nothing but twinkling stars.

CHAPTER 4

D oreen placed a breakfast of scrambled eggs overlaid with processed cheese on the table in front of Bud who was sipping black coffee, absorbed in his newspaper. It was 6:50 a.m.

She put her hands on his shoulders and gently rubbed his neck, kneading the tension out of his muscles. He reached up and touched her arm. They'd had so little time alone lately.

"How many kids today, Bud, will be getting into trouble, drinking, not giving a darn about school?"

Bud sighed. "Too many. And the numbers are growing. Not enough supervision. Most start out as good kids but they end up influenced by hoodlums and dragged into all kinds of risky activities. I'm seeing kids from good homes getting into serious trouble or worse, getting badly hurt." He rapped his knuckles on the table. "That's why it is important for you to be here when the kids get home from school. They need a stable environment where small achievements are rewarded and the day's disappointments are discussed. Most importantly, being home gives you the opportunity to find out what kids they are hanging out with."

"I agree, fully," Doreen said. "I want our free-spirited daughters to hold onto their childhoods as long as possible even if it means extra loads of laundry." She laughed. "And I have a suggestion that I think will work. Are you willing to hear it?"

"Maybe.... All right, let's hear it."

"A small story, before I begin. I mentioned to the BC Tel operator, when I was waiting for her to put my call through, that I had a little spare time now that all the kids were in school. She told me about Avon, a company that sells cosmetics door-to-door. They use women as sales representatives. She gave me Avon's telephone number and address. I sent them a letter a couple weeks ago."

Bud sucked in his breath.

Doreen continued, "I received a reply from their head office in Montreal yesterday."

"Oh gosh!"

"Let me finish." Doreen lowered herself into a chair and faced him. "A representative from Avon will be in town next week and they are holding a meeting at the church to discuss the responsibilities of an Avon representative, the cost to sign on and the challenges and rewards of doing the work."

His frown deepened.

"I want to go, Bud. The kids are all in school and the meeting is only a couple of hours so I will be home in plenty of time to make supper."

"A meeting is one thing. What's the long-range plan?"

"Here is how I think the family will benefit," said Doreen. "Helen is fifteen years old. She is having her little tantrums, right? Not communicating and she puts on too much makeup. Am I right?"

"You don't need me to answer that."

"Once I start with Avon my plan is to slowly involve Helen in it too! She can set her own sales goals and she will have something positive to talk to her friends about. She will learn to apply her makeup correctly and as time goes on she will also earn some spending money for herself. Most importantly, this will keep her busy after school and strengthen her self-esteem. Jane and Andy won't even know I'm out of the house because I will always be here when they get home. I can set my own hours and if someone is sick I don't have to leave the house. And as for me, well, it would give me a way to feel useful now that the kids are all in school." She paused and took a breath. "How is my idea so far?"

"I understand what you're saying, but have you considered how you will get around to all the houses?"

"On foot. That's the beauty of it. I plan to make a few connections each day. I won't know how big it can get until after I try it." She looked up at her husband. "So... what do you think?" she asked, hopefully. "Are you in support of me going to the meeting?"

Bud looked down at his eggs. "Fine," he said at last. "I guess there isn't any harm in a meeting."

"I knew you would understand, Bud! If things go well they have incentives that would allow me to earn bonuses and other rewards...."

He put up his hand. "Whoa, you're getting ahead of yourself, Doreen. I don't want you enrolling in anything until we know more about what's involved and the cost."

"I promise!" she said, grinning ear to ear and jumping to her feet.

Doreen's image of herself trudging from door-to-door was suddenly replaced by a vision of herself cruising around the neighbourhood in a spanking new car, windows down, music blaring, hot-pink kerchief flapping in the breeze. She had seen the image on Avon's recruitment material.

Bud stood to accept his wife's embrace but the sound of kids coming down the hall killed the moment. He shovelled some eggs down and gulped the rest of his coffee standing in the middle of the kitchen. As the three children passed him on their way to the table, he attempted to pat each one on the head. Andy submitted sleepily but the girls took a wide berth around him. He placed his cup carefully in the sink and walked out of the house.

He put the key into the ignition and turned on the car. He listened to the unusual whirring noise coming from the engine. The old BelAir he bought in 1957 sure didn't run like she used to. It had taken him six years to pay it off. He backed the Chevy out of the driveway and began navigating down the quiet street trying to brush from his mind the image of Doreen strutting out the door, valise in hand, while he and the kids sat down to a cold supper. Why couldn't she be happy with the way things were? And yet... how long had it been since he'd seen that kind of joy on her face?

He couldn't help but think about when they'd first met at the Grandview Lanes Bowling Alley while in high school. They'd both grown up in East Vancouver but she'd lived in the Italian enclave near Parker Street and Victoria Drive while he was from the Renfrew area near the Pacific National Exhibition grounds. In fact, Doreen wasn't her real name; it was Doriana, a name that was unique even for Italians. She had always had to explain her name to other kids and spell it for her teachers and so, at the age of eleven, she decided to "English-ize" it, as she explained to her heartbroken Nona. She may have succeeded in changing her name way back then, but her Italian feistiness had remained intact.

The senior boy's year end bowling league championship had just ended with Bud's team, from Templeton Secondary, beating out the Britannia team to claim the coveted trophy. A large contingent of students from both schools had come to watch and were descending upon the bowlers. Bud had seen Doreen at other extramural events and their eyes had met more than once. He found himself searching the crowd for her and spotted her among a group of girls consoling their crestfallen classmates.

"Hi, my name's Bud. I don't think we've met but I've seen you around."

"Hello Bud, I'm Doreen," she replied. "Congratulations on the win. You throw an impressive curve ball."

"Thanks. Sounds like you know the game. Do you bowl?" he asked.

"Only with my family. I'm not in a league."

He picked up a ball and handed it to her.

"Goodness," she said, blushing. "I'm wearing a skirt."

Then she walked over to the lane, held the ball up, and deftly threw it down the alley, finishing her stroke with a sideways flick of her leg and a flip of her skirt. Bud watched in astonishment as the 10 upright pins crashed into the pit.

"Holy Crow! Can you do it again?"

She picked up another ball, took aim and blasted off another strike. Pushing her unruly chestnut hair from her face she looked up at him with shining eyes.

"You're quite a gal."

"Yes, I am," she said, flattening out her skirt.

Eighteen months later, they were engaged.

Remembering who he had married, Bud shook his head.

Quite a gal, he thought as he pulled into the police lot and crossed to the station swinging his heavy lunch box.

CHAPTER 5

" Jane…. Miss Stewart…." The teacher's voice and a few snickers from students woke her from her reverie.

Miss Perkins was staring at her from the front of the classroom, colourless lips pressed into a tight line of disapproval. Another thirty pairs of eyes bore into her.

Jane blinked. "Can you repeat the question, please?" Heat rushed to her cheeks.

"Can anyone here assist Jane?" called Miss Perkins. "Who can tell her, for her further edification, what we were discussing?"

"Cumulonimbus clouds," piped up Tony Brown, kicking the back of her chair.

"In particular, my question was: what kind of weather are cumulonimbus clouds associated with?"

"Would you like me to answer, Miss Perkins?" said Tony. "I believe I know the answer."

Miss Perkins ignored him. "Jane, would you like to answer, or would you like Anthony to answer?"

Jane liked science class and found the topics interesting. The problem was she found it difficult to pay attention to Miss Perkins hopelessly going on and on, taking ages to explain topics that were so succinctly described in the science text. "Rain, hail, wind – sometimes but not always accompanied by lightning and thunder," she replied, seeing in her mind's eye the paragraph she'd read the night before. "I wonder if there can ever be lightning without thunder or rain?"

"Very good," Miss Perkins said. "The answer to your question is maybe. Tony, stop kicking the back of Jane's chair!"

The snickers turned to outright laughter.

Get me out of here. Jane looked hopefully at the clock at the front of the classroom. It was only 9:45!

Before too long she was back in her own world, pondering the flashes of light that seemed to be coming from deep within the forest. They were continuing. Not every night but often enough. They were clearly not storm related as they happened most often when the weather was clear. She poured over the newspapers for any reports of fires or cosmic events, for comets or asteroid showers, anything out of the ordinary. One night over dinner she asked her parents if they were aware of any plans for new streets or houses to be built on the forestlands. Perhaps the lights were from survey equipment.

"Unlikely," her dad said. "That's Crown land. It will always be a forest."

"What about criminals? Could any be hiding out down there?"

"I doubt it. Serious gangs like to be in urban areas where they can sell their drugs, and teenaged thugs usually hang out near the schools or at playgrounds, hoping to come across younger kids to intimidate. Why do you ask?"

"No reason," she replied.

She had decided not to mention the flashes. Some phenomenon was at work and she wanted to get to the root of it, but alerting her parents would bring unacceptable consequences. The last thing she wanted was for them to impose restrictions on her investigation.

She began to record the flashes in her notebook. At first, back in April, there had been a single flash each night around 9:15 p.m. Then, towards the end of the month, there had been nights with two distinct flashes, approximately a minute apart. Now that it was May, two flashes were occurring consistently, and they were happening later each night. Last night the first one came at 9:27 p.m. Before long full darkness would not arrive until close to 10 p.m. Would the lights continue to move to a later time as the days grew longer? And these were just the flashes she could see; it was possible that they were also happening during the day but weren't visible due to the sunlight.

Every evening, before the moon rose and cast its feeble light over the world, she was ready and waiting at her window. She memorized the indistinct outlines of the highest peaks in the mountain range along with the dips, valleys and exposed rock faces, to give her reference points as she waited for the light.

FLASH!

There it was! 9:29 p.m. Two minutes later than last night. Just as predicted. And coming from the base of that mountain... probably along one of the hiking trails. She knew that from her bedroom she could only theorize. If she wanted to learn more, make serious headway, another approach would be necessary. It was time to call in the infantry... I need foot soldiers!

※ ✕ ※

The next day was Saturday, and Jane decided to discuss the flashing lights with Clara, on the condition that she wouldn't mention any of it with her parents. She knew this was asking a lot of her friend. Mrs. Sagan closely monitored Clara's activities and held her to exacting standards at school and in everything else – including her choice of playmates. Jane was keenly aware Mrs. Sagan had sized her up and concluded that her academic strengths only marginally outweighed her many shortcomings – disobedience, inattentiveness, impulsivity, risky behaviour and who knew what else. Who cares, she thought as she walked along the sidewalk, as long as Clara is allowed to hang out.

Clara readily agreed to Jane's terms and listened with fascination and admiration to her theories about the flickers of light and her plans to uncover the cause.

And so, while Rosie plunged ahead through the leafy salal and sword ferns, the two girls scanned the forest. This wasn't just romping in the woods. Jane was on a mission, hoping to find clues that would lead to the source of the light and validate her powers of observation and deduction. For Clara, it was an escape from the constraints of parental supervision and a chance to spend time with her amazing friend.

CHAPTER 6

Doreen arranged a ride to the church with her friend Esther Wilson. She told Esther that she was going to a meeting about Andy's summer camp, not wanting to share her real plans. No need to foster competition for her new business.

Walking up the path to the arched doors she felt a little guilty about using a facility that she didn't really support. The sensation quickly vanished as a polished and perfumed Avon representative greeted her. So sophisticated, no, professional. Glancing around, she was pleased to note that none of her neighbours or other "school moms" were in attendance. She took a pen from her purse and as the meeting got underway opened her notebook and began scribbling.

Once the presentation was over and all the questions had been answered the Avon presenter invited interested women to sign up and purchase a starter kit. Doreen was first in line. Charged with adrenalin, she handed over a cheque for $15.95. Well, we'll just have to eat a few more hot dogs this month, she mused, as she calculated what would be left in the family grocery account.

She walked home preoccupied with thoughts of her new career. Soon she would be setting out into the neighbourhood to call on prospective customers. What would she wear? In her mind's eye she thumbed through her closet identifying a few older but timeless dresses and some smart blouses. Only as she approached her driveway did she remember her bargain with Bud. Oops... well, what's done is done.

Once inside the house she carefully emptied her kit onto the kitchen table and separated the products into categories – cosmetics, cleansers and fragrances. She sampled some of the lipsticks on the side of her hand and used the cold cream to remove the swatches of colour. She was drawn to a brocade perfume package which she unwrapped. Inside was a small glass bottle. She lifted the crystal lid and brought the perfume to her nose. Its floral fragrance transported her, and she couldn't resist dabbing a little behind her ears. Heavenly….

Knock, knock.

"Fuller Brushes," said the man standing on her stoop. He was wearing a cheap suit and scuffed shoes and a broad smile. His puffy face was red and moist with perspiration from the spring heat. In his hand was a large black suitcase. "I am in your neighbourhood this week and thought you might be interested in our new product line of premium hairbrushes."

Doreen had no need for any brushes, certainly not the expensive, heavy black ones being offered, but she felt a pang of sympathy for this man now that she was about to embark on a similar career. She chatted with him pleasantly for a few minutes before declining his offerings. His beaming expression faded into a look of disappointment, or was it despair? She instantly felt guilty. Perhaps she had taken too much of his time. She ought not to have given him false hope.

"Well, perhaps I could buy a nice comb, or something," she offered.

The salesman brightened. "Oh yes, we have some fine ones – top quality plastic!"

Once she had picked the least expensive comb and paid for it the salesman thanked her and turned to leave. Then he appeared to have second thoughts and faced her again. "Do you know if anyone is home during the day in the old house up the way?" He pointed in the direction of the Mason house. "There's a car in the driveway, but no one answered when I rang. I'm wondering whether I should give it another shot."

"I honestly don't know," Doreen replied. "Mrs. Mason is very quiet but as far as I know she is around."

"Maybe I will give it another try," said the brush man as he walked off.

Doreen was encouraged by the spring in his step and by the overall encounter. Her own line of products was much more diversified and exciting than hairbrushes.... Not to mention, more appealing to the women who will be answering the door. If that guy can make a living, just watch what I can do!

In the kitchen doorway she stopped in her tracks. Sophie was on the table hungrily licking up the lilac cream cachet while Rosie stood below, sniffing inquisitively.

"Oh, no, no!" shrieked Doreen as she rushed to save her precious products. "Scat!" She clapped her hands together. "BOTH OF YOU!"

Sophie leapt up in shock, sending ointments and potions cascading to the floor as she scrambled to gain traction on the slick surface. A container of talcum powder flew over the edge and spewed its contents onto the startled dog who knocked the table leg hard as he started to run. The table rocked furiously and almost in slow motion more bottles were upended and started glugging out their aromatic contents. Airborne clumps of Sophie's grey fur descended gracefully and settled on the oily slick covering the table and surrounding floor.

"BAD DOG! BAD CAT!" she called after the animals, knowing they were already far out of earshot.

CHAPTER 7

Helen's eyes flew open. What woke her? Her parents, of course, speaking in harsh tones in the kitchen – nothing new. She quickly put it out of her mind. Felt like she'd been tossing and turning all night, but the clock radio only said 11:30. She was worried about the new cheerleader dance she had to perform Saturday at the senior boys' basketball tournament. She was the only girl on the squadron that kept messing up on the new jump/spin. She just had to get it right. Bobby Leeson would be there watching and she would be totally mortified if she blew it right in front of him. She had been practising over and over but couldn't seem to get it right. So frustrating and demoralizing! She'd been trying to get Bobby to notice her for months and this would be the perfect opportunity. She thought she had caught his brilliant blue eyes watching her at the last game but wasn't absolutely sure. Maybe he was actually looking at Annie, the pixie-like strawberry blonde bouncing around behind her. The spring dance was a month away, so not a whole lot of time to get his attention and an invitation to be his date. She could picture herself wearing that pale blue and white polka-dot dress she'd spotted in Woodward's downtown when her mother and grandma had taken her shopping a few weeks ago. Actually, it was more like window-shopping since they had just looked and didn't end up buying anything. What a wonderful time she'd had, not really thinking about money, and amazingly they'd let her wander around on her own!

Most of the time she didn't feel like talking to her parents. They were infuriatingly over-protective and wouldn't let her stay out past 9:30, even with a group of friends. She was fifteen years old and very mature! Everyone else's parents were so much more reasonable.

Anyways, back to the polka-dot dress and Bobby.... She prayed her parents might help her buy it. She had a little baby-sitting money saved up and clearly didn't have anything else decent to wear. Her mom did hint earlier that a contribution towards the new dress was a possibility if things went well with her new job. Judging from the strained voices down the hall, things were not looking hopeful. So Plan B. She and Deb would make their Home Ec sewing projects into outfits for the dance. The biggest obstacle would be getting their designs past the super-conservative Miss Twist. As for hair, she would do it in a beehive, just like Annette Funicello's in *Teen Magazine*. And with something borrowed from Mom's product samples, her makeup would be perfect. Hmm. Medium-blue shimmery eye shadow with black mascara along with the Pink Baby Doll lipstick, or maybe the Platinum Silver shadow with the Gypsy Cherry red lipstick. Well, she didn't have to decide right now.... Oh, Bobby was so damn cute... she loved how his chocolate curls fell across his forehead. And he was tall too! Most days he dressed pretty cool but not so much in that purple gingham shirt he wore once to English class where he sat one row over and a couple of seats ahead of her. She had taken the seat behind so she could admire him without being too obvious and it was working, she had memorized all his mannerisms and habits and they were adorable; except his flirting with Annie, that was the exception.... Oh, and that purple shirt, yick....

She was also a bit worried about what she and Deb were going to do for their project at the science fair. They had left it to the last minute because Deb had been ill and now the first draft was overdue. Oh well, they could always skip the preliminary class feedback which was optional. It would all be fine... not much time, but Deb was great at coming up with ideas at the last minute...

Finally, she fell back to sleep.

CHAPTER 8

Doreen was anxious but she told herself it was excitement. She had been practising setting up her Avon display for days and was now familiar with all the products in her kit. She was determined to make three calls today. She softly closed the front door behind her and headed out. She had paid special attention to her appearance. If she was going to sell Avon, her makeup needed to be perfect. She had also chosen her outfit carefully, a simple navy blue skirt with a cream-coloured blouse. Her hair, which badly needed a trim, was harnessed in a neat bun. Look attractive but relatable, she had learned at the meeting. Customers needed to believe that they, too, could feel better with a little foundation to even out the skin tone, a touch of rouge and a hit of colour on the lips. A light dab of perfume and *voila...* you will feel as good as you look! When we look good, we feel good.

As she pushed open the front gate at Mary Ellsworth's house, butterflies gathered in her belly. She should not be nervous, she told herself. Mary was a good friend and looking forward to her visit. Nonetheless, it was her first call as an Avon Lady.

❈ ✕ ❈

With a deep sense of accomplishment and brimming with new confidence Doreen strode down the street. Her call on Mary had been so much fun and she had received an order for a lipstick and the signature moisturizer in the beautiful pale-green container. Her first sales! No one was home at the Smith house but she left a pretty pink calling card, promising to return. The next house belonged to the Mason family. She did not know Margaret Mason well but she and George had lived in the neighbourhood for years. Their twin boys went to the same high school as Helen and Jane, although they were one year behind Helen and one ahead of Jane.

The house at the end of the long gravel driveway was one of the oldest structures in the area, built during the days when the North Shore was mostly home to shipyards, fishermen's huts and rustic cabins for outdoorsy townspeople. A few of the old houses had survived including the two-storey former hunting lodge that was now the Mason residence. As Doreen crunched up the driveway to the door, the butterflies started up again. She rang the doorbell and adjusted her skirt.

An upstairs curtain rippling caught her eye. Was someone looking down? Then the door creaked open and George Mason's face peered out at her. Older than Bud, she'd always thought, but possibly that was due to the receding hairline and thin build. His facial features were pleasant enough.

"Good afternoon, Mrs. Stewart."

Expecting Margaret, she quickly collected herself. "Hello Mr. Mason, how are you today?" Flashing her best smile, she went on. "I was hoping to speak with Margaret. I wanted to share with her some wonderful new products from Avon that I think she might be interested in."

George stared at her for the briefest of moments and then opened the door wider. "Call me George. Mr. Mason is my father," he said, smiling warmly. "That is very kind – and ambitious of you. Avon is a good company. But you know, Mrs. Stewart – may I call you Doreen? – sales is a tough occupation. I should know, I have been in sales with Electrolux for over fifteen years."

"Well, that's an excellent company too. Bud and I can't

afford those expensive vacuums, but I hear they are very high quality." She felt herself blush but kept going. "Avon is quite different. Its products are very diversified and priced so that the lady of the house can buy a small treat for herself and stay within the household budget."

"Great sales pitch, I have to say," said George. Then he dropped his cheerful expression. "Unfortunately, Margaret has not been feeling well. She is upstairs resting."

"Oh, I'm so sorry to hear that," replied Doreen. "Is there anything I could do to help? Perhaps bring over supper later?"

"Very kind of you but that won't be necessary."

"Well, I hope she feels better soon." Doreen turned to leave.

"Wait, would you like to go through your presentation with me? I'd be happy to offer some pointers, if you don't think that is too presumptuous of me."

"That would be wonderful," she said, unsure but not wanting to cause offence.

George stepped aside and motioned for her to enter.

She scanned the house as George led the way through the entrance hall, past the staircase and into a dark sitting room. The curtains were open but the north-facing windows brought in little light. The furniture consisted of an overstuffed three-seater chesterfield, two antique armchairs and a set of walnut nesting tables with white rings etched onto their once lustrous finish. On the floor against the wall was a stack of boxes stamped Electrolux in large letters. The smell of cabbage mixed with stale cigarette smoke made her vaguely nauseous. And, good grief, now perspiration was trickling down her arms, disproving Avon antiperspirant's claims of reliable, all day, protection. You're here now, she told herself, just shape up. She took a deep breath, sat down on the sofa and began her well-rehearsed spiel.

"Good," George pronounced when she was done. Then he explained how she should pause in her presentation to let her words sink in, how to tell when a customer is about to take up loads of time without buying anything and how to close a deal as soon as someone shows interest. "And here's a trick." He suddenly put on a hangdog expression which took her aback. Smiling once again, he said, "That look will make the target feel sorry for you and guilty so that they end up buying something small but with a high profit margin." He chuckled. "Honestly, some guys earn a living off that expression alone."

"Very clever," she said with a forced smile. Damn that slimy brush salesman and his stupid comb!

Half an hour later she was almost skipping down the driveway. Her first day and she had made $8.00 in sales – a profit of $2.00! George Mason had bought a small bottle of Lily of the Valley toilet water for Margaret on top of all that good advice. What a great beginning!

CHAPTER 9

On the morning of the school science fair Jane called on Clara. They were partners in a project to study the effect of caffeine on the growth rate of seedlings and today Mrs. Sagan would drive them to school along with the three large poster boards displaying their data, so they could set up for the evening. Doreen had sent Jane along with some home-made coffee cake as a thank-you for driving.

Mrs. Sagan frequently checked her rearview mirror and talked nonstop. "If the concepts are straightforward and well-presented and the conclusions are logical, a project should progress to the district level of the competition. As a former zoology major, I know. And in my opinion your charts and graphs are suitably impressive, without being so perfect that my involvement is obvious. Are you girls feeling confident?"

Mrs. Sagan always amused Jane. But poor Clara, having to deal with that every day. Fortunately, the actual work of exposing, nurturing and measuring the five sets of pea and bean plants had been done at school, on the science lab's large windowsill, away from Mrs. Sagan's manipulations.

Upon hearing about the project Bud had said, "You did what to those poor plants?"

"We exposed them to varying amounts of caffeine courtesy of Nabob instant coffee," Jane said.

"Know what I think?" he joked. "You could sell the ones subjected to the largest doses to CP Rail to use as spikes."

Jane rolled her eyes. Dad was always talking about railways and last year on summer vacation had even taken the family to see the Last Spike in central B.C., explaining with enthusiasm that it marked the completion of the first trans-Canadian railway. Helen had registered her disinterest by refusing to get out of the car. Jane had wondered aloud what their father saw in the funny little shrine. Only little Andy gave it thoughtful examination. "Attaboy," said Bud.

Jane was only mildly interested in the growth rate of seedlings, but she and Clara had dutifully monitored and charted the little green things for the past six weeks. Unknown to anyone, on the same windowsill, hidden behind a cardboard partition and the curtains, a secret experiment had been going on. They'd treated a few seedlings to milk and sugar along with their instant coffee. To Jane, the clandestine nurturing and careful measuring of these secret plants had made the whole project far more interesting. Secrets were so fascinating.

The saddest, strangest thing had happened last week, though. One morning she'd found the seedlings tipped over and dried up when she swept the curtain aside.

※ ✕ ※

The science fair encompassed all classes in the school from grades eight to twelve. The girls set up in the gym that afternoon then went home. After dinner the entire Stewart family climbed into the car and Bud drove to the school for the event. Grade eights presented first, then nines and tens in no particular order, followed by the seniors.

Mrs. Sagan chatted up the judges and introduced the two girls. "Now Jane will guide us through their data and report on their conclusions."

A small audience of parents gathered closer.

"So… we used five different concentrations of coffee, dissolved in water, ranging from zero in our control group, to a maximum amount of four tablespoons per pint," Jane said in her best classroom voice. "After six weeks of observation, we concluded that the presence of coffee, in any concentration, had no effect, deleterious or otherwise, on the growth rate of young pea plants. However," she continued, "in contrast to the peas, the bean seedlings showed measurable increases in growth with weekly watering using the coffee mixture, and those getting the higher concentrations exhibited the greatest growth. Our findings are charted on these graphs and we believe further research will show that they are statistically significant and reproducible."

The parents murmured appreciatively.

"While our experiment concerns simple plants," Jane went on, "our findings are noteworthy because they call into question the widely held belief that coffee drinking stunts growth in children."

That was Clara's cue. "So guess what?" she almost squealed.

The audience members looked at one another but no one spoke up.

"We shared our results with the Coffee Institute of Canada and received a Certificate of Appreciation together with five pounds of coffee." Clara let out a wild giggle and Jane gave her a stern look. "Which we donated to the school staffroom," Clara finished in a rush.

When the applause ended, Mr. Grieves, the school principal, took the microphone. "Thank you, Jane and Clara. Very good work. And, I am pleased to announce, the girls have been chosen to take their project to the district fair in two weeks' time."

Both sets of parents beamed with pride while Mrs. Sagan surreptitiously handed the girls 25 cents each.

Meanwhile quite a few people were gathering at the other

end of the auditorium. The girls nudged each other and escaped their parents and the data boards and made their way to see what was happening.

Helen and Deb were addressing their own small crowd. Their poster read Optical Illusions by Avon.

"Lipstick shades create illusions," Helen was saying, "and can dramatically alter your appearance. Dark colours make the lips appear thinner, reds and oranges focus attention on the mouth, while pale pinks and neutral tones allow the focus to shift to other facial features, such as the eyes. And of course, it's super important to match your lip colour to your outfit for the best all-round effect. Allow us to demonstrate."

Then both girls ducked behind a privacy screen.

Good grief, Jane thought.

She looked around at the gathering, which was now made up of mostly male students, a few teachers, and some concerned-looking parents. Her mom and dad had made their way over and stood at the back craning to see. She cringed when Helen and Deb reappeared. While out of sight they'd applied mauve-tinted frosted lip gloss and switched out their white blouses for clingy plum-coloured sweaters. They posed, pushed their lips out into pouts, turned and posed again, giving the crowd a chance to fully appreciate the remarkable effect of mauve lipstick but also the new marvel of the lingerie industry, the "Cross Your Heart Bra" with its trademarked promise to "Lift and Separate."

Gasps and whispers came from the crowd as Deb launched into a description of the awe-inspiring transformation that could be achieved with an application of Tickle Me Tangerine matte lipstick paired with a frothy mango-hued scarf.

The judges quickly stepped in and wrapped things up to a smattering of applause.

Relieved that the assault on the family dignity was over, Jane ducked into a booth lined with black cloth punctuated with yellow lines and complex diagrams. She was too close to the diagrams to make sense of them but she didn't care as the booth was providing excellent cover.

"I liked your project," came a soft voice from close behind. She turned. Scott Mason was looking at her earnestly, his deep brown eyes set off by ivory skin and collar-skimming light-brown hair. She was surprised to realize that she was pleased to see him.

"I heard you and Clara are going to Districts," he said. "I hope you win your section and go on to Regionals."

Jane wanted to say more but all she could muster was, "Thanks."

"I liked your sister's project more," came a loud, abrasive voice. "Or should I say, your sister's projections." Jim Mason was leering at her. He pushed aside his brother and leaned into her, forcing her to take a step back, pinning her against the display table. "Ha," he laughed, "going to the Districts with your pathetic little garden, so what. I heard your secret experiment went to shit." He smirked at her.

Jane was shocked. Her mind reeled as she tried to make sense of his remarks.

"Cut it out," said Scott, pulling his brother away.

"Who's gunna make me? You? My dinky little brother?" Jim punched Scott's shoulder. "Anyway, we're going to Districts too."

"He means I am," said Scott. "Asshole."

Jane looked around at the yellow lines, then at Scott. "That's great, Scott. What is this project?"

Before he could respond, she felt a powerful force take hold of her arm and yank her abruptly out of the booth. She instantly recognized the overwhelming presence of her father. He was dragging her and Helen through the crowd each by a hand and Helen, too, was struggling to keep her balance as they were marched toward the emergency exit.

"You didn't see this coming?" Jane muttered under her breath.

"Shut up, Jane!"

Bud yanked Helen's arm. "You shut up, Helen! Both of you shut up!"

Doreen was bringing up the rear of the family exodus, looking incredibly stressed and pulling Andy along by his hand.

"Where are we going, Mom?" he asked. "Why are we leaving? I don't think the fair is over, Mom. Where are we going? Did something bad happen, Mom?"

No one spoke on the ride home although Helen was sniffling quietly in the back seat.

"Everyone to bed," Bud directed when they were back in the house. "Move!"

"Why is everyone always picking on me!" Helen wailed as she ran to her room. "It's not my fault that Deb got sick and I had to come up with the project at the last minute."

Jane went upstairs while her mother started putting an unusually co-operative Andy to bed. Doing his part to restore family harmony, she surmised.

She lay on her bed listening to the latest tense exchange between her parents. Her mood was spiralling down. Sophie tiptoed into the room and leapt deftly onto her stomach. "OOF!" She grabbed the cat and hugged her, burying her face in soft fur for a few seconds before the kitty gracefully extracted herself and settled at the bottom of the bed, safely out of arms' reach. She flicked her tail once and stared at Jane.

It was still early, not even 9:30 p.m. and Jane was not tired enough to sleep. She turned on her side and gazed out her window. It would be at least half an hour before the flashes arrived. She reached for her book and was about to open it when inspiration seized her. She could slip out of the house. Undetected. Her parents were far too preoccupied with their argument over Helen to notice. And they'd recently given up their nightly practice of checking on her when they thought she was asleep. So it was possible – a foray into the forest after dark!

She jumped up, tingling. Sophie leapt off the bed.

"Thank you, Helen!" she mumbled. "You're as crazy as a coot but useful nonetheless."

CHAPTER 10

Jane stood outside her bedroom door and listened.

"This is all your fault, Doreen. Bringing all this make-up and woman's lib nonsense into our house. Look at Helen tonight...."

Good, they were still in the kitchen. She stepped inside again and eased her door closed. Poor Mom. Her father was being so hard on her these days. No time for these thoughts right now. She pulled a sweater over her head then put on her runners. She mashed her pillows into a human shape and shoved them under the covers. Just in case. Careful not to make any noise, she pried open the window and unfurled the rope ladder her father had attached to the sill in case of fire. She climbed out and, one foot after the other, two rungs at a time, glided smoothly down. She jumped the last few feet to the ground, landing with a crunch on a mat of dry twigs and leaves.

She crept slowly away from the house, hoping no one would see or hear her. As soon as she was out of the lights, she bolted across the lawn onto the driveway and down the road and did not stop until she reached the edge of the woods. Fuelled by adrenalin, she felt completely alive. As she paused to catch her breath, she surveyed the forest looming in front of her. The trail, so familiar during the daytime, was now a shadowy tunnel; a silvery moon, its beams filtered by the canopy, provided the only light. If this had a been a plan she would have brought a flashlight but tonight was not about planning. She steeled herself and stepped into the gloom.

A soft wind pushed from behind as she walked and the sway of the huge trees with their outstretched limbs seemed to gesture for her to continue farther down the path. Anxiety pricked at her but she pressed on, knowing that this was the mystery. She was in the mystery. She was solving the mystery. She pushed the hair from her face and tucked it behind her ears, straining to see the path ahead. After a few minutes she stopped and took stock. She was deep in the woods but had no way of knowing how close she was to the source of the light. She looked at her watch; the hands on its luminous dial said it was 9:50 p.m. Her heart started pounding and her palms felt clammy as she realized that light would be flashing any time now. She sat down on a log to wait. The woods were deathly quiet; there was only the whisper of wind caressing the treetops. Time slowed to a crawl as she checked her watch repeatedly.

After ten minutes nothing had happened.

Five minutes more.

Nothing.

But why? Was it happening somewhere out of sight? Was she in the wrong place? Hardly surprising since she had no idea where to look or even what to look for.

The damp night air penetrated her sweater, and she started to shiver. She stood up and wiped the bits of bark from the seat of her jeans. There was nothing to be done now except get back home before her parents discovered she was missing.

She decided to run, the pull of home suddenly irresistible. The path was narrow and winding but she could see it ahead a few yards at a time. Once she started running, she could not stop. She ran faster and faster, exhilarated -- no, terrified-- propelled down the path by menacing shapes and sounds. A black shape lurking by the trail! Phew, only a dead tree... A ghostly murmur from above! Oh, just an owl.... Footsteps! Are they my own... or is someone chasing me?

Over-confidence in her agility had tripped her up many times in the past and sure enough her foot caught on a root, sending her sprawling to the forest floor. Her right knee began to sting. She rolled onto her back, drew it up to her chest and rubbed hard through torn jeans. Looking up, all she could make out was the outline of dead looking branches arching over the trail with only a fragment of moon shining through. The darkness was almost complete and she didn't like it one bit. Then, as fast as the blink of an eye, a bright light momentarily illuminated the canopy and brought the branches above her back to life. Shockwaves surged up and down her spine. This was exactly what she had been hoping for! She sprang to her feet, straining to see, but now the forest was darker than ever. Another flash any second, she reminded herself. But minutes ticked by and the forest remained inky black. Had the moon played a trick on her? No, moonlight was never that bright. Whatever it was that had lit up the forest a moment ago held the answer to the riddle she'd been trying to solve for weeks. She had to find it. She replayed the flash in her mind's eye. The intensity of the light had been strongest to the right of the path. I'll just go a few yards in and if I don't find anything, I'll mark this spot and come back in the morning. Then she stepped off the trail and entered the dense woods.

Her progress was hampered by drooping branches, old logs and rubbery saplings pushing hopefully upwards towards the sky. With outstretched arms, she felt her way through the thickest parts. After what seemed like forever but by her watch was less than ten minutes, the forest receded, and she stepped into a clearing. The moonlit sky was open above her. There, in the centre of the glade, was an oak tree, a stranger in this mostly coniferous forest. Perhaps an acorn was dropped here long ago by a bird or squirrel. The scraggly tree looked unhealthy compared to its evergreen neighbours, despite its great height. Some of its branches had been cut, leaving stubs in their place. Her gaze moved slowly up the trunk to the top of the tree. There was definitely something up there. An arc – far too perfect to be a product of nature. If only she could get a little closer.

And she started to climb, stub to branch to stub to branch. Someone had cultivated this tree and done this climb before, probably many times. As she pulled herself upwards, she could see only the thick trunk of the oak and her pale hands as they reached for and latched onto the next branch. She dared not look down. Up up up, she urged herself, until finally, the branches around her began to thin out and she rested for a moment, hugging the trunk. She turned and looked around. She could see for miles. The tree was growing on a slope, its top reaching higher than the trees lower down. Over her shoulder she could see her own house and other houses even farther way. She pictured her parents sitting in the kitchen fretting over Helen, Andy curled up in his bed. What was she thinking, putting herself in this position?

The breeze began rustling the oak leaves and bending the wispy tops of the surrounding conifers. She looked down to the ground so far below. Her hands, grasping the branches tightly, began to stiffen and ache. She felt tears forming but blinked them back. She would have to inch her way down. She was about to loosen her grip and start moving when a blinding light flooded the area, illuminating the skeleton of the tree. Horrified, she tightened her grasp, pressed her cheek against the rough bark and slammed her eyes shut tight. Her pulse was hammering in her head and her knees felt weak. Her thoughts flew to her family. If something awful was about to happen they wouldn't know where to look for her! It was going to be terrible for them. But as she awaited her fate, nothing happened. When she forced herself to re-open her eyes, the light had disappeared, and now all was quiet and still. Relief flooded in. She was unharmed and nothing had changed. She was still clinging to a tree in the middle of a dark forest. Then came curiosity... there had been no sound accompanying the light. How strange.

She peered into the darkness above her. A branch swayed in the wind, and there it was... the arc she had seen from below... and it wasn't an arc, it was a sphere! Looming only a few feet above her was a large saucer-shaped object, at least three feet in diameter and supported by a branch, its back leaning against the tree trunk.

She mustered what felt like the last of her courage and inched higher up the tree, making sure she had a firm grip on each branch. As she got closer, she saw that the object, a near-perfect circle and slightly convex, was strapped to the tree with cables. How could it emit light? There was no source of electricity... no cord running down the trunk to the ground. Perhaps it had a battery.... She reached up and touched the edge of the object. It was cold and hard and so rough that her hand jumped back. Enough for one night! She would come back tomorrow.

She turned and scanned the horizon, seeking reassurance. Her house was right over there, porch and kitchen lights still on, beckoning. A tiny but intense point of light caught her attention. It was brighter than the other neighbourhood lights and flickered erratically – like a deranged firefly. As she watched, it doubled in size and brilliance; then suddenly, the round object was ablaze with light so bright she winced. This time, she forced her eyes to stay open. She saw that everything around her – bark, branches, even her own hands – was bathed in the luminescent greens of the oak's spring foliage. She couldn't help but marvel at the strange beauty of it; it seemed as though she had fallen into one of the watercolour illustrations from her botany textbook. Then, as stealthily as it had arrived, the light darted away and she was plunged back into darkness. Time to get the hell out!

She scrambled down the tree, dropped to the ground and picked her way through the underbrush back to the path. Without pausing, she fled at top speed along the trail and reached the edge of the forest, lungs burning. At her house at last, she flung open the front door and collapsed in a heap on the hall floor next to an overjoyed Rosie. She reached out to him.

"Hey... Rosie, it's... alright," she gasped, "I'm... okay."

Rosie wagged his relief and licked her bloody knee. Beloved mistress; safe.

The commotion drew Bud and Doreen from the kitchen. Bud looked shocked then angry.

"What's going on?" he demanded. "You're covered in twigs. Have you been outside?"

"I was only taking Rosie for her evening walk. You and Mom were busy. I was playing with him and fell on my knee." She pointed to her torn jeans.

"Jane, you were sent upstairs," said Doreen. "But it was good of you to think of Rosie." Doreen put her arm around Jane's shoulder. "We have all had enough excitement for today. Let's get that knee cleaned up and you tucked into bed.

"Yes, Mom," replied Jane.

Back in her room, she hauled up the rope ladder, yanked the curtains closed then got into bed. She pulled the comforter over her head but the blanket provided no warmth. She shivered. What was going on? Her fears swirled and escalated, and sleep would not come.

At midnight answers arrived instead. That thing was a big mirror in a metal casing! The light was coming from somewhere else. But where? And why? She froze as the next thought dawned on her. Someone in the neighbourhood was behind that light. And using the contraption in the tree to direct it into her bedroom. A chill ran down her spine. The mystery had taken a decidedly disturbing turn.

PART TWO

LIGHT

CHAPTER 11

She lay curled on her side, hugging her legs to her chest, her heart threatening to pound its way out of her ribcage. The light was coming from her neighbourhood and being directed by a giant mirror into her bedroom, her private escape from the world. Her life was being invaded. What was she to do? She wanted to run downstairs and tell Helen. But could she trust her? Or would her sister rat her out? If her parents found out she had gone into the woods alone at night and lied about it, she would be grounded for life! But maybe the police should be involved. Maybe there should be an investigation. What if someone was out to get her?

Suddenly another bolt of light, softened by the thin curtains, bathed the room in pink. And it was way past midnight! She did not know how she'd arrived downstairs in her old room, in her sister's bed, but was grateful to be there, taking comfort in the familiar smell of Helen's shampoo. Helen was fast asleep but snuggled anyway. Jane looked at her sister's lipstick-smudged face dimly lit by the porch light outside the window. Then she closed her eyes and settled in, relieved to be back in familiar territory, at least for now.

❊ ✂ ❊

With a slam of the door Bud was gone. He didn't even step into the kitchen for a morning coffee; he'd make do with the bitter brew at the station.

At 8:00 a.m. he was called to the front desk to deal with an unexpected visit from Miss Wright, the girls' gym teacher. Oh great. What was wrong now? What a perfect start to a perfect day.

"Constable Stewart, I stopped by to ask if you would be willing to come to the school next week to talk to the students about the dangers of marijuana. You made a real impression on some of them last year."

"Just doing my job, Miss Wright. But I'm pretty busy these days."

"Please, my name is Candy, short for Candice," she said. "I baked some cookies on the weekend and thought you and the rest of the boys here might enjoy them. The community needs more people like you, Constable Stewart, or if I may, Bud."

He recalled how she had hung on his every word during the last presentation. And smiled at him constantly. She seemed a nice young woman. In good shape, too. Now, as she pushed the cookies into the centre of the desk, he couldn't help but notice her curves in the tracksuit and the long blonde ponytail cascading over one shoulder. He caught the captain's eye as she turned to leave. Nice package. He felt a rush. She didn't need any makeup to look good. Perhaps he could do another presentation.... Then guilt.

❋ ✕ ❋

Helen got dressed in slow motion. Embarrassing, her parents dragging her from the fair like that. Cruel. Could they not see she was becoming popular, she was not a child anymore? Everyone at school would know that she had gotten in trouble. Plus, she was grounded. No phone or television for two whole weeks! So mean. Trying to ruin everything that was important to her just because they were miserable. Unfair!

And when she went to the bathroom to grab her makeup bag it was gone from its hiding place.

⁂

First block was Math which was Jane's favourite subject, but her mind was stuck on the events of last night, especially the discovery of the mirror in the tree. Was it only meant for her or was there another meaning? Who could she talk to? Her dad would have a fit if he found out that someone was using a mirror to spy on her, and her mother was so preoccupied with Helen these days.... Before she could figure out a single Math problem, the bell rang. She wandered out of the classroom into the hallway and turned blindly towards her next class and almost walked right into Jim Mason.

"Look who we have here! It's Miss Darwin, future botanist," he said. "Good thing you like science 'cuz you don't have the looks for a cool job, like you could never be a model or even a stewardess."

She tried to step around him but he moved with her, blocking her path. She wanted to slug him but settled for keeping a straight spine and her head held high. A few other students sent anxious glances her way, but no one intervened. Then Scott appeared from a nearby classroom.

"What's going on?"

She set her mouth and lifted her chin in a show of defiance. "What's it to you?" she said and pushed her way between the boys.

"Ooooh, spunky!" she heard Jim say as she walked down the hall, refusing to look back.

⁂

In the middle of English, while the rest of the class was doing silent reading, she wondered if Clara might help her identify the house that was sending the light to the mirror. But Clara had turned out to be useless at keeping secrets from her mother, having slipped up more than once during the initial phase of the investigation, so she was out as an accomplice. Maybe Helen was her best bet after all, being so upset with their parents, she might agree not to tell. They could work together as a team again. She would take Helen to the mirror in the tree --- it would be like old times, except this time the mystery was real.

At lunchtime the cafeteria was noisier than usual. It was Fun Friday and the cook was serving Sloppy Joes. Jane was exhausted. She could hardly keep her eyes open and wasn't hungry. She skipped the line-up and located her sister at a corner table huddling with the cheerleading squad. Helen seemed transfixed by something happening at another table and, oh no, it was that meathead Bobby. Her sister was making goo-goo eyes at the dumbest guy in the school. Everyone knew he had been held back in grade one and was barely able to manage the non-academic track. But there it was, her sister giggling and waving at him, looking desperate for his attention.

Unbelievable!

Helen's judgment had gone on a leave of absence. Fellow spy? Don't think so. Jane turned with a heavy heart and retraced her steps to the land of Sloppy Joes. Maybe one day they would be friends again but as for intelligent sleuthing together? Not likely. She was on her own.

CHAPTER 12

June already! Doreen was contemplating her to-do list. Mondays and Wednesdays go door-to-door while the kids were at school; Fridays place customer orders with head office, and review product literature and marketing strategies somewhere in between cooking meals, making lunches and beds, and showering. It was a lot but so far her efforts were paying off in the form of a tidy little income. But today her focus would be on domestic duties, in keeping with her promise to Bud. He had been so distant recently.

"Best to get on with this," she said aloud, as she surveyed the mess in the kitchen.

She hand-washed the breakfast dishes then gathered up the clothes from the kids' bedrooms and took them into the laundry room. Mindlessly, she separated the laundry into darks and lights and loaded the machine. She pulled a box of detergent from under the sink and eyed the packaging. A pretty blonde in a flattering sundress smiled out at her, perfectly happy to be doing laundry.... Well, I was pretty happy when I was her age and had that figure... Actually, on closer inspection, she looked a lot like Helen's gym teacher. Bud had spoken to her classes just last week. She felt a pang of jealousy. He had mentioned that she had brought homemade cookies to the station. Were they for everyone or Bud only? After turning on the washing machine she trudged into the bedroom, went to the bureau, and opened the top drawer. From deep under the clothing pile she pulled out the pink frothy negligee Bud had given her on their anniversary two years ago. She had worn it that night and not seen it since. She laid it on the bed and braced herself for what was coming next. She undressed in front of the full-length mirror and forced herself to look. Her once lithe body had been ravaged by three pregnancies, extra weight and poor fitness. Did vacuuming count as physical activity? Nope. If so, she wouldn't look like this.

She gingerly pulled the negligee over her head, found the matching bottoms, and slipped them on too. When she sized herself up in the mirror she found she was pretty happy with how the airy chiffon fabric softened everything. She turned side to side and took in the effect from all angles.

From another room came a loud kerfuffle. Rosie and Sophie were chasing each other across the kitchen floor. "Stop it," she yelled. She peered out of the bedroom doorway in time to see Sophia Loren careen down the hall and skid past her ankles into the bedroom, with Rosie in hot pursuit. The cat leapt three feet into the air with tail and four legs outstretched and all claws extended and landed on the chenille bedspread. When Doreen went to pick her up, a claw caught on the coverlet, pulled out a long thread and caused the material to bunch up. Doreen held the cat down with one hand and with the other tried to pry the nail free from the bedding. At the same time, she used her bare leg to push away the agitated dog and separate the two animals. She felt a wet spot on Rosie's coat. What was that? After releasing the cat, she leaned over and felt the dog's fur. Sopping wet. Had he been outside? But it was sunny…. "Why on earth is your fur wet, Rosie boy?"

Suddenly she remembered. The washing machine… she couldn't hear its usual rumblings. She rushed to the laundry room and found herself wading barefoot through several inches of cold water with more gushing from under the machine.

With quaking hands she picked up the phone and dialed the police station. "Bud, I am in the house and water is pouring out of the wall behind the washer."

"Where exactly?"

"From a big pipe above the electrical outlet."

"Doreen, get out of the house right away!"

"But, but..."

"Do it NOW!" he commanded. "You could be electrocuted. Go outside and stay there until I arrive."

She hung up the phone and ran out the back door with Rosie and Sophie. She sat down on a chair next to the BBQ, with tears streaming down her cheeks. The house would be badly damaged by the water and maybe the appliances would need to be replaced. How would Bud react? They couldn't afford a large expense.

⁂

Bud hit the siren in the black-and-white and a few minutes later skidded to a stop in front of the house. He jumped out wearing full emergency response gear – a florescent vest thrown hastily on top of his uniform, a yellow hard hat and a utility belt around his waist. He pulled up the cover plate in the lawn by the driveway and hurriedly turned off the municipal water line, then strode around the side of the house into the back yard looking for Doreen. He found her crumpled over in a chair, face in her hands. When she looked up her eyes were red and puffy, her cheeks hash-marked with smears of mascara. He breathed a sigh of relief.... But... what the hell?

"Let me guess," he said. "All your other clothes were in the wash?"

She cried harder. "Am I just a mother to your kids now, Bud? Is that what this 'family first' stuff is all about?"

"What are you talking about?" He went to her with arms outstretched, lifted her up from the chair and held her close.

After a moment he set her down and looked into her eyes. "Everything is going to be okay," he said, then added, "That's quite an outfit."

Her sobs stopped. "Do you like it?" she asked, smiling and striking a pose.

"I picked it out, didn't I?"

"Bud," she said turning serious, "I can help pay for the repairs... I'm really good at my job."

"Doreen, you're good at everything you do.... If you want to keep trying this sales thing you have my support. But I have three conditions. One: family first. Second: you can't wear that negligee when you go door-to-door. Third: you will wear it tonight."

They looked at each other and started laughing. Soon they were bent over, snorting loudly, laughing even harder.

Finally, they regained control.

"My stomach aches," said Bud.

"It seems like a hundred years since I've laughed like this," added Doreen.

And they went inside to inspect the damage.

The doorbell rang.

"It must be the plumber." Bud said. "I called him before I left the station."

"Wait!" shrieked Doreen. But it was too late, the door was open and a man in coveralls holding a toolkit was standing on the stoop staring at Bud in his uniform and Doreen in her negligee.

"Uh... okay. Is this what I think it is? Not really my thing."

Bud slammed the door in the man's face and Doreen broke out in fresh gales of laughter.

"You are a nut job," Bud said.

CHAPTER 13

The morning air was heavy with moisture. Jane got out of bed, went downstairs to the bathroom and locked the door. She stood under the hot water and peeled the clingy vinyl curtain from her leg. Running her soapy hands over her body, she felt the sensitive swell of her breasts. Crap, crap... crap. She rinsed off and got out of the shower. With a towel she swiped away the condensation that had formed on the full-length mirror that hung on the back of the bathroom door. Then she stepped back and appraised the misty image of the naked girl standing before her. She had grown taller in the last few months and there were other changes too. Her once stick-straight, lean frame was now softened by graceful curves. Her waist was narrower or at least appeared that way in contrast to her hips which seemed to have grown slightly broader. Uh-oh.

She dressed quickly and forced herself to focus on the day ahead. Clara and her mother had worked hard to get them to the District Science Fair and Jane was prepared to see it through. There would be science exhibits of every kind, demonstrations, questions from the judges, newspaper coverage, and if they won their category they would go on to the Regionals with the coveted $100 first prize. She knew that her parents were proud of her no matter what, but she had decided: if they won she would put her share of the money towards the new washing machine. Anyway, concerns about what her body was up to would have to wait.

At the Sagan's, Clara's mother gave her and Clara individual packs of mint-flavoured gum neatly wrapped in waxy light-green paper and silver foil. They went right into their routine, mimicking the TV ad. "Double your pleasure," they sang, "double your fun." Jane chewed loudly, savouring the treat, a rare thing; Doreen was a firm believer in achievement being its own reward.

By 4:30 p.m. the Centennial Auditorium on Lonsdale Avenue was bustling with activity. Mrs. Sagan, Clara and Jane checked in at the registration desk and then made their way down the second aisle to their assigned booth, D26. So many people, 48 exhibits in total – the best from every high school in District 44. The first hour was general open display and then the competition would start with the judges moving about the room, giving each team five minutes to demonstrate their project and answer questions.

Clara and her mother seemed to have their booth in order so to distract herself Jane wandered off – just to check out the competition, she told herself. Really, she was hoping to find Scott Mason, the only other competitor from Windsor Secondary. Wow, clearly Mrs. Sagan was not the only parent willing to lend a helping hand. And so many complicated thingies, she thought as she walked down the aisles filled with displays. She suddenly lost confidence. All these other projects looked so sophisticated. It was amazing that they'd made it this far in the competition. Sprouts and coffee?

Turning down the next aisle she saw the familiar mop of light brown hair and black-and-white checkered shirt that Scott always wore for special school events. He was standing alone in front of his display, adjusting the layout of his handouts. For some unfathomable reason, she quickened her pace, looking forward to seeing his friendly smile. He was on the lanky side compared to the much stockier Jim, but they were similar in height. He seemed smart, if a little too serious, and had a quiet way about him. He didn't go out for school sports like his twin who was on the rugby and basketball teams, but she had seen him deftly crack a softball into the outfield and make sensational throws to home plate during neighbourhood ball games. As far as boys went, Scott might not be all that bad.

Surprise then recognition registered on his face.

"Hi," she said.

"Hi."

Silence.

This was getting awkward fast. Why hadn't she come prepared with something to say?

"Sorry if I snuck up on you... I should get back to my booth," she said, preparing to abandon ship.

"No... don't go... I was hoping to see you here tonight."

"You were?"

"Ya, for sure. I think you and Clara could win the prize for your grade level. Your method is first rate and your findings are the kind of myth-busting stuff that calls for follow-up research."

New feelings stirred. Pride, sure, but something else was going on. Suddenly shy, she looked away from him towards the bold geometric shapes on the black posterboard behind the display table. This was the booth where she had been before her dad yanked her away. But she hadn't had a chance to digest anything that night. Now she saw the title of the project emblazoned in neon yellow block capitals: THE POWER OF LIGHT / COMMUNICATION IN THE FUTURE.

She studied the display, strong straight lines bisecting the black background before being re-directed upon intersection with a plane. Fascinating. Light projected and then redirected and manipulated around corners. Light manipulated. Her pulse quickened and her ears began ringing. She studied the display, not wanting to believe what she was seeing. But it must be true. It was Scott! He was behind the mirror in the tree! He had been spying on her with some creepy giant laser beam! She turned to face him.

"PERV!"

She lunged at him, putting both hands on his chest and shoving hard.

Caught by surprise, Scott fell backwards, crashing into the brochure table, sending it skidding into the six-foot tri-panel screen separating his booth from the one behind. The screen teetered briefly then toppled over backwards, sending test tubes and pipettes on the other side smashing to the ground. Yelps of alarm filled the air as students and parents scrambled to get out of the way and teachers rushed over to see what was happening.

Shaking, she turned and ran from the auditorium, through the lobby and out into the damp night air.

CHAPTER 14

"My mom is so mad at you," Clara said. They were walking solemnly down the street, schoolbooks lodged in the crooks of their arms.

"I'm sorry," said Jane. "I was so angry last night, I just reacted."

"Reacted to what?"

"Well, it was Scott Mason, the whole time. The flashes of light? His science project was all about lasers and light refraction. He's been flashing that light into my room for weeks. I was so shocked I lost control." Her anger was rising again. "I pushed him but I didn't mean for his whole project to fall over."

"Plus the one on the other side," Clara said. "Have you reported him?"

"No... I don't know what to do. I can't tell my mom or dad."

"Why not?"

"Well, I snuck out at night and went into the woods, remember? I would be grounded for life!"

"I call bullshit," said Clara.

"No, it's true."

"I think you like Scott and don't want to get him in trouble."

"That's a load of crap! I hate him."

"I don't care one way or the other but you got us disqualified! Everyone thought you intentionally damaged another student's work. For both of us to be disqualified after all that work...."

"I know. I'm so sorry, Clara."

"My mom says I'm not allowed to do any more school projects with you. She doesn't want me to hang out with you after school or on weekends either. She says you're too wild... not lady-like."

Jane stopped in her tracks. "And you? What do you think?"

"I don't know. Why do you think Scott Mason is shining a light into your room? Why would he do that? Have you asked yourself?"

"No. I don't know."

"Well, you should."

"Should do what?"

"Ask yourself."

Clara picked up her pace and strode away from her. Up ahead three other grade eight girls were walking towards the school. Clara broke into a run and joined the group. Simultaneously, all the girls turned around and stared. Jane stopped walking and looked left and right but there was nowhere to hide, and it was too late anyway. Shrill giggles wormed into her ears.

A deep rumbling sound from behind announced the Mason family car coming up the road. She moved to the shoulder and shifted her pile of books to her stomach, cradling them in both arms. George Mason was driving his two sons to school. As the car passed, Jim Mason stuck his head out the front passenger window. "Too bad about getting kicked out of the science fair!" He grinned broadly, then threw back his head and began howling like a mad dog. "Owww... Owww... OWWWW! Owww... Owww...OWWW!"

"Stop it," shouted George, taking one hand off the wheel and cuffing his son. The car swerved and then corrected itself. As they drove away, she could see Scott's face turned to look at her through the rear window.

"Morons! Assholes!" She yelled after them. She dropped her books and picked up a stone. Mustering all her strength, she hurled it after the car, which was already too far away. The girls up ahead saw the stone skipping down the road towards them, and suddenly they were all shrieking and running pell-mell down the street like frightened quail chicks, Clara included.

"Oh crap," sighed Jane, watching them go. Her feet seemed planted in the gravel on the side of the road, unwilling to take her to school. She hated Jim Mason and now she hated Scott too. Worse, she had let down her best friend and maybe lost her friendship. Everything in her life was going wrong. Reluctantly, she made her way along the soft shoulder, up the school driveway to the double glass doors, down the hall and through the back door of the class, which was already in session.

"How nice of you to join us, Miss Stewart," remarked Miss Perkins. "Now report to Principal Grieves' office immediately."

CHAPTER 15

Helen rushed through the front door and flung herself onto the couch. She must have an early evening tonight as tomorrow was the start of the playoffs in the Senior Boys Basketball Tournament at Sentinel High and she needed to rest her tired and aching body after practising cheers before school and during lunch every day all week.

Windsor Dukes, what's the scoop?
Put that basketball through the hoop!
Put it up!
Sink it in!
Come on, Dukes, win, win, win!

She pictured herself cheering in perfect unison with the rest of the squad, each step, twirl, squat and, of course, the new jump/spin which had been a daunting challenge but which she had finally mastered. It was going to be absolutely amazing and she was going to be perfect! Bobby would be sitting right in front of her on the team bench with those beautiful blue, mesmerizing eyes. And she was going to get them turned on her! He was just so hunky with his blue-and-gold shorts hugging that tight, muscular butt. Just imagine, someday soon, they could be embracing each other, their bodies pressed together while a French kiss sent them both into paradise.

She decided to pass on dinner, must not over-eat. Plus, she needed to iron her skirt and top, pack her bag with replacement cosmetics, hmm... must remember her new bra, she would need that for sure. She grabbed a bag of cotton balls from her mom's Avon supplies. Should do the trick. By 9:00 p.m. she was fast asleep, meeting Bobby in her dreams.

The next day's classes were uneventful but then she wasn't

really paying much attention. The school bus would be leaving promptly at 3:45 p.m. for Sentinel. Right after the final bell rang, she met Deb in the washroom and they changed into their cheerleading outfits and put on their makeup. Helen whipped out her bag of cotton balls and proceeded to stuff her bra a bit at a time, taking a moment to bounce around after each adjustment to make sure the truth wasn't exposed. Deb giggled and encouraged her to keep adding more. One last glance in the mirror and it was time to join everyone at the bus.

Joey, Michael and Fred were hopping around in the parking lot like they had ants in their shorts. They were like the Three Stooges, always hamming it up. Last year they pulled full-moons out the window of the school bus right after the district finals. Lucky for them they didn't get caught. So juvenile.

Maybe there'd be a chance to talk with Bobby on the bus but maybe it would be better to wait until after the game was over because they both needed to concentrate on what lay ahead. Besides, on the way to games the team always sat together to build team spirit, whereas going home the students were allowed to sit wherever they liked. She would try, with Deb's help, to be in the right place at the right time – beside Bobby for the ride home. He would smile at her and say how amazing she looked and what a good cheerleader she was....

The bus got on its way filled with excited chatter punctuated with outbursts of hooting and cheering. Sentinel Hilltoppers, one of the better teams in the tournament, had three wins and zero losses so far. Tonight, the Dukes were going to break that streak.

Windsor Dukes, what's the scoop?
Put that basketball through the hoop!

✠ ✗ ✠

Jane car-pooled to the game with one of the volunteer parents who took student spectators to away games. She was looking forward to the event but was also more than a bit worried about her sister's uncoordinated cheering after watching her practise in the backyard.

She picked a seat off to the side in the bleachers and looked round. Scott wasn't on the team but he sometimes came to watch. Tonight he wasn't in the stands. Good! Also, she didn't want to end up with Tony behind her making wisecracks or poking her in the back. She had just gotten settled when the Windsor Powder Puffs and the Sentinel Sweethearts trotted into the gym, ready for action, pompoms in their school colours held tightly to their waists. Most heads turned to watch as they took their places along the sidelines. Jane was enjoying the scene too – until she heard someone whisper, "Look! Isn't that the same girl with the Avon products at the science fair?"

Oh my gosh. She could not believe what she was seeing. Helen's boobs stood out like twin volcanoes ready to erupt. What was she thinking? Thank goodness Dad and Mom aren't here!

✠ ✗ ✠

The boys raced out onto the court as the announcer called their names. The cheerleading squadrons cheered their players on, and the spectators roared their support; the whistle blew and the game began. First quarter the game went back and forth with the teams keeping within four points of each other. It was going to be a tight game.

Then, during a time-out, it was the cheerleaders' turn. The

Sweethearts went first and to Helen's eye they were low-energy and unexciting. She was happy because that would give her team, and her in particular, a chance to shine. And now it was time....

She noticed Bobby staring at her. She put on her best smile, lifted her chin high, whipped her shoulders back and strutted out to the gym floor in almost perfect unison with the squad. The music was surging through her veins. She put every ounce of herself into the routine and danced like never before. Bobby's gaze never faltered. Fireworks were going off in her head! The whole crowd was yelling and whistling by the end of the routine. She looked for Bobby again and saw approval on his smiling face. He didn't care that she'd blown the kick/spin.

A whistle blew and the game resumed. Bobby was at the very top of his game, his body glistening with sweat as he scored basket after basket. Sentinel surged ahead by six points. But Windsor came back to tie it up as halftime approached. The cheerleaders took to the floor again. Helen's eyes found Bobby and, whoops, she found herself a little out of step with the routine. Annie elbowed her in the side and gave her a "snap out of it" look. She re-focused, finished the cheer and was back on the sidelines, when Bobby rushed by dribbling furiously towards the basket to break the tie! A Sentinel player fouled him sending him crashing to the gym floor. The referee's whistle blew and Bobby was getting two free throws! He walked up slowly to the free-throw line directly in front of her and expertly swooshed both shots up and into the basket. She jumped to her feet cheering and clapping as the entire Windsor crowd went wild. The noise was deafening, super-charged by the desperation of the Sentinel players who were now down by two points. Helen stepped forward waving frantically. She was mesmerized and saw only him. "Way to go, Bobby!"

"LOOK OUT!"

Was someone yelling at her?

A powerful blow knocked her off her feet and unhooked the band harnessing her chest. A boy twice her size careened away into the bleachers while spectators yelped and scrambled out of the way.

Helen lay on her back on the gymnasium floor, gasping for breath.

The referee and concerned parents moved quickly towards her but some players were there first. A pair of strong arms lifted her up and then placed her carefully on a nearby chair.

"Are you alright?" a voiced asked.

The room was spinning but she was able to nod. "I think so… but what happened? I thought it was a time out."

"No, it was an inbound play, there's no break in the game after a penalty shot."

As the crowd around Helen grew, the referee signalled the half-time break and the players were shooed away to the locker rooms. She slowly looked around. The two large wads of cotton balls had disintegrated into hundreds of individual pieces and were now drifting across the gym floor like cherry blossoms on a breezy spring day. Joey, Michael, and Fred were laughing as they kicked at the white puffs, scattering them far and wide.

She covered her face with her hands and wanted nothing more than to run to the washroom and hide. Then she was seized by a realization – Bobby had picked her up. He had held her in his arms so gently and shown real concern. Oh, the firmness of his grasp and the smell of his sweat. Oh! A little drum started thumping in her chest.

As she retrieved a few cotton balls from her top and started wiping her cheeks, she noticed that her sister was there and looking at her with concern.

"Are you okay?" asked Jane.

"Fine," Helen said. "Did you see?"

"Wish I hadn't."

"Bobby picked me up!" she said happily.

The game ended 72–60 for Windsor with a loud burst of applause and hoots of delight. Twenty minutes later the players and cheerleaders piled onto the bus. Helen abandoned Deb and bolted straight to where Bobby was leaning forward with his forearms braced on the seat back, chatting with the guys in the row ahead.

"Hey there, Mr. MVP," she said, taking the empty seat across the aisle.

Bobby looked at her and broke into a grin. "Well, if it isn't my favourite cheerleader. You really took one for the team there. I don't think that Sentinel kid ever got his head back in the game."

"All part of my ploy, you know."

"Every last detail?"

"Yes." She paused. "The details. All those details."

Everyone laughed, Helen loudest of all.

Bobby turned his attention back to his buddies and they proceeded to go over the game play by play, laughing and cussing as the bus made its way back to the school.

She had to think of something clever to say but she was struggling. She was about to say, "I love how you dribble," but before she got the words out Bobby turned to her.

"Helen," he whispered, "I hope you're going to the spring dance and we can meet up there."

A blast of joy detonated in her chest. "Yes, I am planning on going," she was quick to reply.

With a twinkle in his eye and a big wide smile, he added, "By the way, I'm more of a leg man."

CHAPTER 16

The stench of formaldehyde soured the air and two dozen bovine eyes stared at her unblinkingly from a glass jar as they awaited their fate at the hands of the next day's biology students. Jane wrinkled her nose. Better get used to this kind of thing, girl, if you want a career in health sciences. She was serving out the last day of her detention, cleaning up the science lab at the end of each day. Clara had been spared since she had not been responsible for the damage at the fair. Too bad, Jane mused, missing her. She went over to the window and saw Clara with her new friends walking down the school driveway to the street. Clara had become distant. She had even changed her seat in science class to a desk far from Jane's. Jane held her breath and worried. Would Clara tell her parents about the lights and the mirror in the tree? So far nothing had happened. So far Clara was keeping her confidences.

Her thoughts turned to Scott. It was his fault she had been stuck here until 4:00 pm every day for the past two weeks. Unbelievable! His weirdo light experiment, a mirror in the tree, invading her private space.... What a creep! He was worse than his asshole of a brother... and to think she once thought he was nice.

On top of everything, her parents were upset with her over what happened at the fair and her reluctance to explain herself. Normally she didn't keep secrets from them but this time was different... she had let things go too long... telling them now would make things worse. She would just have to weather their disapproval.

✠ ✄ ✠

The halls were abuzz with students scurrying to their lockers and talking excitedly about the Spring Fling dance on Friday. When the bell announced five minutes to the start of last block Helen grabbed her garment bag from her locker and hurried off to Miss Twist's home economics class. The teacher must have thought the students were all colour blind. The colours she had suggested for their skirts were Pepto Bismol pink and canned cream corn yellow. Really? Helen made a production of pulling out her flame-thrower yellow poplin, waving it like a cape in front of a bull. Deb had chosen siren fuchsia for her fabric – a choice that screamed "look at me and go blind." It was satisfying to watch Miss Twist's involuntary shudder when they whipped out their fabric and started work. The ultra-conservative teacher's nostrils flared just like Jane Goodall's chimps. Wow, first a bull and now chimps, she was on a roll.

"How old do you think Twist is?" whispered Helen.

"About ninety."

"I know, so wrinkly. But what about her hair?"

Once the sewing machines were set up with colour-coordinated thread, the girls began sewing the casings for the elastic waistbands to be inserted on the almost finished skirts. Once completed, the skirts would satisfy the sewing portion of the curriculum. The only thing left to do after this was hem the skirts according to Miss Twist's strict length requirements. Most girls would re-hem them at home to make them into minis.

When Helen's thread tangled in the bobbin again, Miss Twist marched over like a sergeant and took charge of the machine.

"Helen, pay attention. You must learn how to do this

properly. How are you ever going to cope as a housewife without basic domestic skills?"

Helen rolled her eyes at Deb and leaned in close to watch the rescue operation.

"There, you see?" said the teacher, rising from the chair. Unfortunately, her immaculately coiffed blond hair remained behind, tethered to Helen's wrist by the silver unicorn on her charm bracelet. As she fumbled to help untangle the mess, Helen stepped on the sewing machine's power pedal and the machine lurched into action. Before anyone could stop it, Miss Twist's glossy up-do was in the throat of the machine being sewn tightly onto the offensive canary dirndl skirt complete with bright yellow stitching.

What??? No way!! The two girls exchanged looks of horror.

As the teacher tried frantically to tug the wig free, the other girls in the classroom looked over at the commotion. Their mouths gaped open. Miss Twist wears a wig! Laughter bubbled forth like shaken soda-pop. An ear-piercing shriek could be heard throughout the two-level wing of the school as the bald Miss Twist abandoned her flossy locks and fled to the staff room.

The following day, Helen and Deb performed a successful wig-ectomy, painstakingly removing the hairpiece from the cherished garment. Since no one was supervising, Miss Twist having called in sick, they gleefully adjusted the hems of their skirts so they only just skimmed the edges of their new hot pants. Altogether an excellent outcome as far as they were concerned.

❊ ✕ ❊

Friday afternoon at last! After the bell rang, the girls stuffed their skirts into their gym bags and headed off to Deb's house to get ready. They laid out their tools on her bed as meticulously as surgeons. On one corner was their artillery of pilfered products from Doreen's Avon samples: foundation, rouge, eye shadow and false eyelashes. On the other corner was a tangle of fishnet stockings and the newest thing going, pantyhose in many shades, thanks to Deb's mom who worked in the hosiery department of Eaton's Park Royal. A rainbow of neon-coloured polyester crop-tops occupied the centre of the bed and on the floor at the foot of the bed lay a pile of gently used go-go boots and pointy sling-back shoes scrounged from the local thrift store.

"This is the definition of heaven," said Helen.

"No kidding," said Deb, setting up her mother's ironing board. "First, we need to flatten our hair. After that, makeup and then we get dressed!"

"Oh no!" said Helen.

"What?"

"My dad! Miss Wright asked him to chaperone tonight! He'll go ballistic when he sees me!"

Deb snapped her fingers. "I have an idea," she said. "You can wear a disguise. I brought home Miss Twist's wig and my mom helped me fix it so we could give it back." She pulled out the crumpled blonde wig from her dresser drawer and held it up. "See, it's quite long and pretty. It just needs to be ironed out. Plus, we can cut in some bangs. No one will recognize you."

A few minutes later Helen was trying it on.

"It's perfect!" said Deb.

"Really?"

"Truly."

"You're not just messing with me?"

"My goodness," exclaimed Deb.

"What?"

"You're a dead ringer for Miss Wright!"

Helen looked in the mirror. Deb wasn't kidding. The resemblance was remarkable; they were about the same height and weight. Wow. What a transformation! She'd never felt more beautiful and grown up.

※ ✕ ※

By the time the girls sashayed out of Deb's mom's car and up the steps to the school they were brimming with confidence. They looked perfect, right down to daisies painted on their cheeks. First they ran into Joey, Michael and Fred.

"Who's the babe with you, Deb?" asked a gobsmacked Joey. Helen breezed past with a haughty jut of her chin. Then, when they were at a safe distance, she turned wide-eyed to Deb.

"They really didn't recognize me!"

Soon they were surrounded by the cheerleading squad. Emily, Susan and Daphne gushed over them, agog.

"Where did you get the fishnets? Are those fake eyelashes? Where did you get the wig? Can you paint our cheeks too?"

And then Annie walked over and looked Helen slowly up and down. Everyone held their breath. Annie had always been her rival; they'd competed in soccer, gymnastics and now cheerleading. Ever since they were small, Annie had always got the better of her. And lately, with her remarkable chest development, Annie was getting all the boys' attention.

"You look... absolutely amazing!" she declared. "Can I also have a daisy?"

All the girls, including Helen and Deb, squealed with delight.

"Yes! We have enough extra body paint and makeup for everyone. But let's wait for intermission, the band is about to start."

Helen headed into the gym with her spirits soaring. The excitement was nuts. The art students had outdone themselves with the Flower Power theme: beautifully crafted papier mâché flowers strung up with psychedelic lights overhead. And everyone was dressed up in "love and peace" regalia. The senior girls had fixed the ballot so that everyone could wear outlandish outfits and staff had no say, and there would be a prize given out for the best-dressed girl and boy. She was the sure winner. Tonight she was outshining even Annie! She felt supercalifragilisticexpialidocious!

The lights on the stage came on and the band started up with *She Loves You.*

Yeah!

⁜ ✕ ⁜

Bud cringed when he saw girls with dates gyrating en masse on the dance floor while shyer girls stood around the edges of the room with their friends hoping to be asked. By the third song, when they abandoned all hope and danced with one another, he began to relax.

The volunteer parents had done a superb job with the refreshment table set up on the east side of the gym. This was his station for the night. He sauntered over to dip into the non-alcoholic punch bowl which was still three-quarters full. Meanwhile the cases of coke and 7-Up were being downed at a rapid pace. He was relieved to see that the teachers and other parent chaperones had made an effort to dress up, to fit in. He was feeling a bit less like a dork in his hippy attire. Mr.

Klassen, the science teacher, was wearing paisley and even Principal Grieves had on a tie-dyed shirt. Doreen was absent due to an Avon event with a bunch of cackling women, but she had put out some clothing options for him. It really was her responsibility to be here tonight but no, she was committed to doing yet another Avon party. Too bad Andy was at a sleepover or he would have had the perfect excuse to say home and watch TV with him.

Ultimately, Jane had persuaded him to put on the ridiculous outfit. She had been recruited to hand out drink tickets and dressed the part in Helen's green shift dress accessorized with a single strand of beads. Dresses were not her favourite so seeing his youngest daughter's commitment to the cause, he had reluctantly donned the fringed leather vest, jeans and aviator glasses. He even let her tie a braided headband around his forehead.

"See, Dad? You're really fitting in," she said, crossing the floor to check on him. "You could be one of the cops on Mod Squad!"

He stuck his thumbs in his vest. "Groovy."

"What happened to the peace-sign necklace, officer?"

"Left it with the flowered shirt. Not my bag."

Jane flashed a peace sign and faded into the crowd. Bud felt his mood brighten. One of the other chaperones was supposed to be Miss Wright. Where was she?

※ ✕ ※

From the other side of the gym Helen was keeping an eye on her father by the refreshment table. Thank goodness for the blonde wig and the dim mood lighting. It was obvious her dad had not recognized her and she wanted to keep it that way.

Deb's mom was picking them up after the dance and the plan was for her to sleep over at Deb's house. Just keep away from Dad for a couple of hours and – ah, there was Bobby, and he was staring straight at her.

Emboldened by her new look and the spiked sodas consumed in Deb's bedroom, she skipped over to him. "Hi!"

"Hey baby, whatcha got cookin'?" he said.

"Something special," she said with a mischievous air.

Bobby sized her up then leaned in and said under his breath, "You're a big upgrade from the chicks at this school."

"It's me, Helen," she proclaimed, stopping him from going further down the road he was on.

"Helen?" He did a double take. "Ha, just kidding."

"The hell you were," she said.

Bobby gave her his big smile. "Wow! Helen, you look super hot!"

To her amazement and delight, she felt a new power rising within her. She could use it, she could render the gorgeous Bobby Leeson powerless – any boy, for that matter. They would be putty in her hands.

On cue, Joey, Michael and Fred hooted in unison from halfway across the floor. "Hey Bobby," yelled Joey as the three started towards them, "introduce us to your hot new friend!"

Bobby looked at Helen. "Meet me behind the bleachers after the intermission."

Before the trio of boys reached them, Helen and Bobby were headed off in opposite directions. She glanced knowingly over her shoulder to see that he was doing the same. She was bursting to find Deb and tell her the news!

❈ ✄ ❈

Bud had settled in. He was a cop after all and this was basic surveillance. He surveyed the gym, checking all exits and entrances and satisfying himself that all in the crowd of youngsters was okay. He found he was enjoying himself and tapped his foot to the beat of the music. Miss Wright looked exceptionally lithe and athletic and, well, attractive. At his classroom talks to her students she was always dressed in a tracksuit. But tonight, whew-ee, those legs in that short skirt went on forever! And her hair... long and luscious, released from its usual elastic, draped like gold silk over her shoulders and down her back.

But something was amiss. She had greeted him warmly when he arrived, but ever since had been dancing with some girls, and scooted away every time he tried to approach her. Women! Never figure them out. He was looking forward to Andy getting older so they could catch the odd game at Nat Bailey and have a few beer together. He looked out over the crowd doing its thing on the dance floor. Thirsty work, anyway, doing nothing. And it was getting very warm. Must be from all the gyrating bodies in a closed space. He decided to open the gym doors to let in some fresh air. The rule was no one was allowed to leave the gym and then come back in. A smart school policy to prevent alcohol consumption. Since the open door was immediately behind the refreshment table he could sneak out for a quick smoke and still keep an eye on things. He smoked his cigarette while enjoying the cool evening air.

Glancing back into the auditorium he saw Miss Wright dipping her cup into the punch. He called out a greeting and started walking towards her but she slipped back into the crowd. And then, for a moment, he thought he was seeing two Miss Wrights. Was he seeing double? Had someone spiked the punch? He shuffled awkwardly from foot to foot trying to decide what to do – stick or twist. Stay here or try and have a word with her. Just an innocent word or two. No harm, no foul.

❈ ✖ ❈

At 9:30 p.m. the band returned from its break and started on their final set. Helen was in ecstasy. It was time for her rendezvous with Bobby. Student voices sang in unison, almost drowning out the band's cover of *I'm a Believer* as she danced the Funky Chicken through the crowd toward the back wall of the gym. Love was no fairy tale tonight! With a quick shoulder check to see if anyone was looking, she ducked under the bleachers. All year she had been focussed on getting to this point and now here it was. Her dream date with Bobby.

❈ ✖ ❈

Bud noticed a figure that looked like Miss Wright scooting along the back wall of the gym. Did she just go under the bleachers? Now here was an opportunity. He signaled for Mr. Klassen to take over his post then made his way across the gym floor to the stands. He peered under the structure but the psychedelic light pulsating between the risers made it difficult to see anything clearly. Filled with uncertainty, moisture forming on his palms, he stepped into the shadows. What am I doing? Ah, there she was… But?…What the heck? She was with a boy!

"Miss Wright?"

"Oh my God! DAD!"

"What? … Who's there?

"…It's me."

Who's me? Wait a second, he knew that voice!... "Helen?"
Silence.

"Helen, is that you?"

"Er, yeah."

He froze in his tracks, eyes locked on Helen, who flickered
in and out of view in the strobe light. She looked like Miss
Wright but with a ridiculous yellow flower on her cheek. And
she was with that Bobby guy! A switch flipped in his mind
and he couldn't stop the daggers flying from his eyes, daggers
usually reserved for criminals.

Bobby turned and ran off like he was being chased by two
burly forwards.

"What's going on here!" came the voice of Mr. Grieves from
behind.

"It's the principal!" yelled a voice from deep within the
cave.

A dozen amorous couples disengaged and took flight. In
the stampede of sneakers and kitten heels, the reams of duct
tape pinning down the electrical cables were yanked free. As
the students tripped, fell and scrambled to get up, the force
was transmitted along the cords to the line of amplifiers on
stage, causing one of them to crash onto the gym floor with a
flourish of sparks and a deafening shriek of feedback. Then
the transformer blew – the music stopped abruptly and the
gymnasium was plunged into darkness. Horrified screams
filled the air only to be replaced, seconds later, by hooting and
cheering as the students rejoiced in the chaos.

Bud, shaken and fumbling, retrieved his police whistle
from his vest pocket and blew repeatedly.

"Everybody stay calm!" Mr. Grieves commanded as he
headed off to start up the auxiliary power.

The Windsor Spring Fling was over.

CHAPTER 17

The school year ended with the usual assembly and handing out of scholastic and athletic prizes. Scott Mason won the grade nine science prize. Clara earned a certificate for perfect attendance, then she flew away. Sent to stay with her grandparents in Manitoba.

The house was unusually quiet these days. Doreen was either out selling Avon or working away in the kitchen on the administrative side of things. Bud of course was always down at the police station. Andy was at church camp and Helen usually headed off to Deb's or the mall. Feeling abandoned, and without Clara to hang out with, Jane spent the first week of July with Rosie exploring the creeks and gullies in the forest. Until the rain set in. For a full week, heavy grey clouds delivered relentless showers, turning the woods into a bog fit best for amphibians. Her mood sank along with the barometer. She wandered around the empty house looking for inspiration. She experimented half-heartedly with yeast, watched bread rise. Billions of microscopic fungi collaborating energetically to puff up the dough, showing off how great it was to have friends. Mocking her. She studied the complex threading system and tension mechanism of her mother's sewing machine until she understood how they worked together to moderate the repetitive jerks of the needle and produce a neat line of stitching. Impressive. Too bad people didn't come with tension control dials. Hers needed adjustment.

Now she lazed on her bed leafing through one of the comic books Andy left strewn around the house. The stories were lame but the pages were filled with colourful graphics depicting muscular men and a few women engaged in extraordinary feats of strength and endurance. Many possessed superpowers to aid them in their battles against evil, but she favoured those with human vulnerabilities: Batman, Ironman, Spiderman. They were smarter and braver than the likes of Superman who was pretty much invincible, or that Nordic Neanderthal, Thor, who flew around cudgelling everything with his magic sledgehammer. Bruce Wayne, Tony Stark and Peter Parker had to enhance their athleticism with ingenious gadgets to defeat their enemies. She respected that resourcefulness.

She was drawn to one character despite his minimal human characteristics. The solitary Silver Surfer first appeared as a minor character in the Fantastic Four magazines as an intergalactic sentry for a higher, alien power. He was humanoid in form but as silver and glossy as mercury and he glided effortlessly across the Universe on a metallic surfboard. Unlike other superheroes, he wore no special suit of clothing. In fact, there was nothing at all covering his form which was slender and not overly muscular. Otherworldly but beautiful. He rarely spoke. He was an outsider, like herself. An introvert in a galaxy dominated by extroverts.

With Donovan's melodic voice straining to be heard through the tiny speaker of her transistor radio, she studied the Surfer closely and found herself tracing the outline of his form with her fingertip. She closed her eyes and imagined what his skin would feel like, wondered what he would look like life-sized. What if he could glide his surfboard up to her window and visit her. What would they say to each other? Would they find the need to talk at all? She brought her legs together, crossed her ankles and squeezed her thigh muscles. Zing! Wow. That felt good.... This puberty thing had an upside worth exploring!

❊ ✂ ❊

The catastrophe at the Spring Fling had upset Doreen and she and Bud had been at odds ever since. Why hadn't she been there? What really happened? Did he have a crush on Miss Wright? And what was that garbled explanation all about? After that weirdness he just wouldn't talk about it. Why? And what a ridiculous name, Candy. It sounded like that spun sugar crap sold at the PNE.

But, ever self-critical, Doreen wondered whether the whole thing had been her fault. Was she letting her job interfere with her family responsibilities? If that was the case, she was willing to adjust. She decided to cut back her door-to-doors from twice a week to just once. That would free up an extra afternoon for the preparation of meals. No more pork and beans with toast for dinner! In addition she would reduce the weekly Avon parties she hosted to every two weeks. Avon products had become very popular with the neighbourhood moms, thanks to her; and with new houses springing up all around and more families moving in, the demand for products could be expected to grow. Nevertheless she would dedicate more of her time to domestic responsibilities. Family first, always.

Bud, when she told him her decision, looked pleased but also a little ashamed.

Chapter 18

The rain had finally let up and the morning sun was gleaming in the sky like a gold medal. Jane could hear normal weekend sounds in the house – Rosie barking at Sophie, her dad cursing the overflowing coffee maker, her mom scolding him. She ran downstairs – "No breakfast for me!" – leapt onto her bike and headed out. The air, warm and moist with humidity, acted like a tonic and her spirit soared. In her backpack she had half a dozen books she had finished reading and were overdue at the library. If she got there when it opened and pleaded forgiveness in person, she might avoid the fine and pick up some replacements. After peddling hard to pick up speed, she stood on her pedals and coasted down the hill. The closest thing to flying. She was preparing to swerve around a large puddle on the edge of the road when she noticed a person walking uphill towards her. It was Scott. She hadn't seen him since the assembly and now there he was, right in front of her. She would show him! She tightened her grip and steered directly into the puddle. A second sense said danger – but it was too late; something clutched at her front tire. The bike came to a sudden stop and she was pitched over the handlebars into a mass of twigs and wet leaves. Damn it!

She struggled to get up but the bike had landed on top of her and the books strapped to her back weighed her down even more. And now Scott was leaning over her. What a disaster. He was supposed to be the one covered in mucky water, not her! She had tried to put him in his place but here she was, splayed out on the road, humiliated.

Scott carefully lifted the bike off her and set it aside, then offered his hand. After a moment's hesitation she took it and pulled herself up.

"You okay?" he asked.

"I guess." She shrugged, looking down at herself. The palms of her hands were scraped and bleeding.

"Looks like you hit a clogged drainage grate."

"I know what I did, you don't need to tell me."

"Right. How is your bike?"

"Seems to be okay."

"You could both use a bath," he said, grinning.

They walked together up the road, Scott wheeling the bike.

"You know what?" he said.

"Why don't you just tell me?"

"I'm sorry for what I did. You know... the lights... I knew you would be intrigued and would try to figure it out."

"Figure what out? That you're a creep?"

"That they were a signal."

"A signal?"

"The lights... It was just a kind of test at first, I guess, part of my science experiment. I wanted to explain it to you at the science fair but with Helen's antics and all the commotion I didn't get the chance."

"So explain. What signal were you trying to send?"

"I guess... maybe... something to interest you... so that we could... um... become friends."

"Good grief! There are easier ways."

"I think you're the smartest girl in school, maybe the smartest person I've ever met. I never meant to scare you," he said softly.

"Scare me? You almost killed me! I found your tree and almost fell out of it. If I had fallen and died, how long would it have taken for anyone to find me? Can you imagine what my parents would have gone through?"

"You climbed the tree?" Scott asked.

"Damn right I did, in the middle of the night, when my parents thought I was asleep."

Scott's jaw dropped.

With a surge of pride she saw that he had completely underestimated the curiosity and courage of Jane Stewart. But he should have anticipated she would end up in the woods at night. What an idiot he was! It was such a stupid, stupid thing to do. And yet.... She looked at his stricken expression. It was obvious he was devastated. She could see his self-doubt. She could also see that he had meant what he said. Of course, he hadn't meant to harm her. Did he also mean what he said about her being the smartest person he'd ever met? And about wanting to be her friend? He might be overly quiet and for sure was lacking in a certain follow-up thinking, but maybe he wasn't all bad.

"It was a pretty cool mystery," she said eventually.

"It was the dumbest thing I've ever done," he replied. "But I hope you realize that I couldn't see into your room. I wasn't spying. It was just a light show. But I'm truly sorry. I won't bother you again...." He handed over the bike and started to walk away. "And I don't blame you for trying to splash me."

"Wait."

He stopped and turned back.

"I accept your apology," she blurted. Just saying the words lifted a weight off her shoulders.

Scott stared as if he didn't believe what he was hearing.

She slowly nodded her head. "I do. I forgive you." The words made her heart swell in her chest. It was as if she had been freed from some invisible cage. She took a deep breath and savoured the feeling of lightness that was flooding over her. Was holding that grudge, not the rain, the cause of her blahs? She could see Scott was too stunned to react. But soon, she saw relief welling up in his eyes. It was strange how such a simple exchange of words could change everything. Something hopeless had ended; was a new beginning possible?

"Really?" he said, looking directly into her eyes.

"Yes." She gave him a smile.

"Can I check on you? To see how you're doing? Sometimes you're more sore a day or two after an accident."

"Sure," she said after a moment of hesitation.

"As for my experiment," he said. "I could have been expelled for what I did. So, um, thank you for not reporting me."

"Your project was excellent," she replied. "A sure winner. Just a bit misdirected in the testing phase." They continued walking together up the street towards their houses. "So... tell me how you did it. How did you get the light to flash into my window?"

His eyes brightened. "It's not that complicated. I broke into that junk yard behind the shipyards and got a headlight off an old truck, then I connected it to a twelve-volt battery my dad had at the house. After that I positioned a lens, kind of like a magnifying glass, a few inches in front of the headlamp to concentrate the beam of light and keep it narrow as it travelled to the tree. Without it, the beam would have been so wide by the time it hit the tree that the light hitting the mirror would have been too weak to make it all the way back to your window. To finish off that part of the set up I attached a toggle switch so I could easily turn the light on and off. After that, all I needed was a reflector but it had to be a substantial size and set up at just the right distance. I looked for a climbable tree tall enough to clear the rest of the forest and that oak tree was perfect, just over half a mile away. Of course I had to adjust everything a gazillion times so that the light hit your house, then your window.... I was never quite sure I was hitting the target or that you had seen it. It was only when you shoved me at the science fair that I knew for certain. I was just trying to put into practice some of the ideas from my physics project. And it worked!"

"But... car headlights only light up the road for a short distance, nowhere near half a mile. How could you make the light travel so far?"

"Right... that's true. A headlight on low beam will only illuminate the road for about two hundred feet, high beams let you see around three hundred and fifty feet ahead. But that's different from the distance from which you can see the beam. You can see the light coming from a headlight at night from more than a mile away if it's pointed in your direction."

"I get it," said Jane. It's like how you can see buildings at night if their lights are on. Like how we can see the lights of downtown Vancouver even though its miles away.

"Or even farther. Think of the sun and stars and how far away they are, yet their light is visible from Earth. And while we're talking outer space, think about the Moon. Moonlight is nothing more than a reflection of the Sun's rays, right? The Moon has no independent energy source and yet it sends out light, just like my mirror."

"Yup, very cool...Tell me about the mirror."

"So, the reflector is an aluminum garbage can lid with a circular mirror mounted inside. I got the lid from the side of the road and banged it into the right size with a hammer. I found the mirror at a garage sale. Part of some lady's vanity table, I guess. Mirrors make excellent reflectors as they absorb only minimal amounts of light. Anyway, I cleaned them up real good, put them together... and PRESTO, I had a reflector. After that I trimmed away some of the tree's branches and strapped the reflector to the trunk with old phone cables."

She looked at Scott with admiration. "That's bloody brilliant! Wow... light from an old truck headlight was coming from your bedroom and being redirected by the mirror into my room?"

"Right," said Scott.

"Still very creepy."

Scott laughed. "I'll call on you!" he said as he left her at the end of her driveway and walked backwards up the street towards his house, maintaining their eye contact.

CHAPTER 19

In late July, out on her revised routine, Doreen called on Mary Ellsworth.

"Hi, Mary, how is your summer going? Too bad about all the rain!"

"Nice to see you, Doreen," said Mary, but not opening the door wide. Not ushering her in as usual.

"I've got the latest Avon products to show you. Some exciting moisturizing creams I think you'll like."

"I'm sorry, Doreen, but Janet was here just yesterday and I ordered from her. I didn't know you were going to be here today, and you know me... if I want it, I'm going to buy it."

"Janet Henshaw?" said Doreen. "Since when has she been an Avon rep?"

"At least a month. Didn't you know? This is my second order from her. She has a great system. The day she makes a sale she sets a date with you for her next visit. You know when she's coming and can plan your day around it. She also keeps a huge supply of product in the trunk of her car. So you don't have to wait as long... oh, and did you know she serves wine at her weekly parties? I think she's doing quite well."

Doreen thanked Mary and walked back to the sidewalk.

Her blood was boiling but she continued, as planned, going house to house. And heard the same story every time. A few former customers simply shook their heads and looked down at their doorstep. She was furious. That woman is moving in on my territory! I'll show her....

But by late afternoon, as she walked home, having failed to make a single sale, she was no longer angry. She was dead inside. When she walked through the front door, she saw Bud standing like a scarecrow in the kitchen. Without saying a word she went straight into the bedroom, slammed the door shut and flung herself face down on the bed.

After a few moments she heard him doing his little shuffle in the doorway.

"Are you okay?"

She buried her head in her pillow and said nothing.

He sat beside her and put his hand on her back. "What's wrong?"

"My business is over.... Please just leave me alone."

After a few moments of silence, she felt him get up and leave the room.

※ ✄ ※

Bud poured himself a whisky then went out to the front step and sat down. Rosie came over and flopped beside him and they both watched the cars going by. All the guys he knew... husbands returning home from work in the city.

CHAPTER 20

The day after the bike incident Jane heard a knock on the front door. She waited, but no one was getting it. She ran halfway down the stairs and stopped in surprise. Doreen was in the kitchen, making no effort to answer the door.

"Mom?"

"Will you get it, Jane?"

She didn't like seeing her mother so disengaged. Normally she would have hurried to open the door and greeted whoever was on the other side with a welcoming smile. That Doreen was not in residence. This Doreen worried her. She knew a girl whose parents had been fighting and ended up getting divorced last year. Too scary....

She opened the door to find Scott standing on the stoop looking awkward. A spurt of delight washed away all other thoughts.

"I... I..." he stammered. "I wanted to see how you were doing."

"Oh, I'm fine," she said. "You didn't really need to check on me—" She stopped herself. "But it's nice that you did."

She stepped outside and closed the door. The last thing she needed was Helen or Andy poking their noses into her business.

Scott went on. "I also wanted to give you this." He reached into the pocket of his grey kangaroo jacket and pulled out a folded piece of white paper. His hand was trembling slightly as he held it out to her.

She took the paper and opened it up. On it was a hand-drawn chart with letters and symbols. She stared down but was unable to make any sense of it. She looked at him enquiringly.

"It's the Morse Code," he explained. "Each letter is represented by dots and dashes. It's a communication device invented over a hundred years ago, around the time of the telegraph. The dots are short blasts and the dashes are longer. They can be used to send signals over great distances, usually over wires."

"I've heard about that," said Jane. "There's a universal call for help, SOS, and it goes dit dit dit, dah dah dah, dit dit dit... and then repeats."

"Right," said Scott. "I thought that you might be interested in learning the code. Then we could...." his voice trailed off.

She stared blankly at the paper in her hand for a moment then suddenly got it. "You are an evil genius!" she exclaimed. "You could send me words! But how will it work? I may be able to decode your messages, but how will I be able to respond?"

"I thought of that. Your dad's a cop. He must have a high-powered police issue flashlight, right?"

Jane nodded. "Sure. He keeps one in the kitchen junk drawer. He almost never takes it out except to make sure the batteries are working."

"You can use that."

"But how? I can't just randomly flash it out my window."

He grinned. "I've already started collecting the rest of the stuff you'll need. The signal won't be as strong as mine but I'll be watching for it so it should work just fine."

"This is the craziest idea, EVER. We do have telephones, you know." When she saw his crestfallen look and the self-doubt returning, she quickly added: "I love it. I really love it!"

Scott's face lit up with joy. She felt it too. She hadn't known it was possible to be so filled with happiness that nothing else in the Universe mattered. This was a moment unlike any other. And it was tinged with sadness too – made her realize how lonely she had been.

❋ ✖ ❋

Bud could barely contain his elation as he drove home. The smell of searing pork chops greeted him as he opened the door. Did this mean things were getting back to normal? He put the keys on the hook and headed straight for the kitchen. Doreen was standing over the sizzling stove. He approached carefully and put his arms around her from behind.

She turned and gave him a puzzled look. "What's this all about?"

"I passed the test for the detective position!" he announced, grinning proudly. "The next step is an interview with the chief."

Doreen smiled but it was forced. "Great. I'm sure that makes you feel good about yourself."

"If I get the promotion, I'll get a raise, not much, but something – and we can both feel good about that."

"Being successful at my job would have done that for me but I'm happy for you."

This wasn't the reaction he was expecting. "I'm sorry your Avon gig didn't work out – all your clients abandoning you, after all the work you put into it. But we are a team, Dory. When one of us succeeds, we both succeed."

"Really? Is that what you think? It's not what you said when I wanted to start working and when the going got tough."

He recoiled. How much anger and resentment had she been

harbouring? "I come in here with good news for the family and I get this as a response? This is bullshit!"

He marched out, stepping over the abandoned Avon sample kit in the hall and slammed the front door. He tromped down the street towards the woods. What the hell. What a bummer. Once on the trail, his heart rate began to slow. He'd get the promotion or he wouldn't. But what was he thinking? Miss Wright? The girls' gym teacher? And blaming Doreen for Helen's antics? A short way into the forest he stopped to light a cigarette and – tap tap tap. He peered up into the treetops. There was a woodpecker up there laughing at him. "Okay, buddy, you're not the only guy here with a self-inflicted headache."

⚜ ✂ ⚜

Scott was true to his word. He brought Jane a magnifying lens and showed her how to position it in front of the flashlight to focus the beam. After that it was trial and error each evening until finally… contact!

During the day they rode their bikes around the neighbourhood and hiked the forested trails. Before long they were spending parts of every day together. Occasionally they went on full-day excursions as far away as Horseshoe Bay or Deep Cove where they sat on the docks watching schools of shiny minnows swim in tight formations and gulls vying loudly for the best bits of edible flotsam. While exploring Mount Seymour they came across a deserted one-room cabin with an old wood stove. The windows and doors were gone but the shell remained intact. The next day they came back with matches and a can of beans and made a fire in the stove. They cooked the beans in the can and shared a spoon. It became a regular destination on days when the summer rain returned. Huddled together away from the elements and prying eyes they chatted about the pressing issues of the day: which was better, *The Man From U.N.C.L.E.* or *The Avengers*, Coke or Pepsi, the Stones versus the Beatles... and their favourite teachers.

"Mr. Klassen, is really cool," Scott said. "He gives me extra experiments to do and, like, more challenging stuff. His first name is Art, as in Arthur – wouldn't it be nuts if he taught Art?"

"Yeah, ha, Art for Art's sake... that would be cool." She carried on, "I think he teaches Socials too. I hope I'm in his class next year."

They both disliked Miss Perkins.

"She could suck the air out of any classroom," Jane said.

"No lie," said Scott.

"What about Miss Wright?"

"Oh, she's, well, she's...."

"Oh my god, you are blushing!"

"Well, I think she is a good gym teacher – she's amazing at track, and she's got a lot of swimming awards...."

"You think she's hot, don't you? ... Is she as hot as Mrs. Peel?"

"No one's as hot as Emma Peel."

"Okay, okay. What do you think about Principal Grieves?"

"Probably a Narc."

"Oh, that's true!" she said. "Trick question. Who's your favourite superhero?"

"The Incredible Hulk."

"Really? What do you like about him?"

"He's a tormented misunderstood genius."

"Like you? Except, he's green and has fits of rage."

"Nobody's perfect. Who's yours?"

"Silver Surfer."

"Why him?"

"None of your beeswax."

After dark, each alone in their respective bedrooms, they had short, truncated conversations. Jane had become adept at hitting the reflector, sending a pinpoint of light to Scott waiting by his window to receive it. He'd respond often before she'd finished sending. And the cryptic messages became their secret language.

"Hel"

"Lo"

"Dins"

"Stew"

"Tomorrow"

"Mac N Ch"

"No what we do"

"Ha creek swim"

"OK how you mom"

"Still sad"

"Too bad nice lady"

"Night"

"See you"

❖ ✄ ❖

Summer dinners at the Stewart house were often eaten on the back patio. Eating outdoors was something everyone loved. Tonight, Jane watched a robin land and dig for worms. A pair of squirrels darted back and forth already gathering their winter stash. It was as if they were all at the same picnic, animals and humans. But this summer wasn't like past summers when Bud and Doreen had been in tune with each other. Tonight, the three kids kept quiet as Bud silently ate his burger. He didn't share his day's work like he used to. And Doreen didn't ask Andy about his adventures or ask what the two girls had been up to. Conversations weren't flowing. Jane tried to help by chatting about the book she was reading, but that went nowhere. She volunteered nothing about her time spent with Scott and downplayed it when asked. Her father would not understand and her mother and sister might get too interested.

After dinner Jane couldn't wait to scamper upstairs to her bedroom. Evenings had become her favourite part of the day. When the last traces of sunlight were gone she knew a flicker of light would arrive signaling the beginning of her nighttime messaging with Scott. She visualized him in his room with his lens pointed towards the mirror, sending beams of light meant only for her, his keen mind focused on the task, his lean, angular frame bending towards the window, towards her. They had found a closeness facilitated by the distance between them and began sharing sentiments they were too shy to express face–to-face.

"I like hanging with you," she signaled.

"Me too."

"You are cool for a brainiac."

"Oh ha, thanks…You are…."

"I am what?"

"…Beautiful."

"…Bull."

"Soon everyone will see it."

After they said their "good nights" her mind returned to his words… No one had ever said anything like that to her before. She was startled by the impact it had on her – by the feeling of warmth swelling within her chest. Beautiful? She had never thought much about it; brown hair and hazel eyes were nothing special. And these were just superficial things, she reminded herself. But as she drifted off, in the margin between sleep and wakefulness, she heard him whisper... "You are beautiful" in her ear.

CHAPTER 21

Wonderful, sunny August! The number of hours between dinner and bedtime had not changed but by eight o'clock the day was almost over, with longer shadows stretching across the landscape. Blackberry season had arrived and the thought of the little flavour bombs detonating in her mouth had Jane's salivary glands aching. She left the house after dinner promising to bring back a supply for the family. She and Scott met up at the end of her driveway and together they headed into the woods towards the blackberry bushes she and Clara had discovered the previous summer. The brambles flourished along certain sections of the trail thanks to splashes of sunshine allowed in by expansive swaths of open sky; telltale signs that the forest had been previously logged, the best firs and hemlocks hauled off long ago to the mills along Burrard Inlet. The huge, disintegrating stumps left behind now played host to young trees, huckleberry bushes and all manner of fungi as the forest sought to regenerate itself.

The blackberry briars were fortresses. The canes were brutally tough and armoured with sabre-sharp thorns designed to deter any would-be invader. Jane always wore long sleeves and pants when picking but inevitably ended up with scratches on her hands and occasionally on her neck if she reached in too far. Maddeningly, the juiciest berries were never quite within reach.

"Blackberry bushes provide sanctuary for small animals like mice and squirrels," she said. "Otherwise, they would be at the mercy of predators like hawks and cougars."

"Un huh," he agreed. "And owls... I've never seen a cougar, around here, have you?"

"No, they're very shy."

"And stealthy... they sneak up on their prey from behind and pounce."

"Hey, don't eat all the berries! They're for my mom's pie."

After picking berries for a while they walked further along the path and over to the glade with the oak tree. They put down their pails, climbed a short way up the tree and hung out on its lower branches.

"The homeroom assignments were posted today. Who do you have this year?" Scott asked.

"Miss Perkins again."

"Me and Jim are in Mr. Klassen's. My brother hates him but that's nothing unusual. He hates everyone. Hey, did you hear that Mr. Grieves has been transferred?"

"No, really?"

"Yah, they say it's because of what happened at the Spring Fling."

"Helen strikes again!"

They laughed.

"Yeah, and there's a new woman principal."

"Way cool!"

As the light faded Jane looked up at the highest branches. No sun. "Time to get going. Otherwise, our evenings together will be over."

Scott jumped down from the tree and held up his hand. She wasn't planning on needing assistance but then her grip failed just as she was about to let go of the branch. Scott tried to catch her but she managed to fall on top of him with her full weight and they ended up in a heap at the base of the tree.

As they disentangled themselves her hip brushed up against his and their hands touched briefly. A fleeting moment of contact yet it was enough to send an electrifying pulse through her body.

They scrambled to their feet. She took a step backward. Scott was now looking at her with concern. "Are you okay? I was only trying to catch you."

She felt the warmth of a blush on her face and realized his deep, brown eyes were reaching in, touching something deep inside. She had to look away.

"I'm fine," she said, brushing off bits of debris.

Chancing a glance up, she saw that Scott had moved a little closer.

"You're not very graceful for a girl. Isn't this the second time I've had to pick you up off the ground?" he said, seriously, before breaking into a wide grin.

His dimples were deep, and his smile so sweet and disarming. Good grief! It's not like she hadn't seen his smile and those dimples oh so many times over the last few weeks. What on Earth – *uh-oh*.

Scott took her hands and gently pulled her towards him. He was no longer smiling. He tilted his head down to hers and looked directly into her eyes. Their lips were almost touching. She felt the warmth of his skin on her face – inhaled the sweet scent of blackberries on his breath. She felt certain that he was going to kiss her but he stopped and slowly drew back.

"I don't want to ruin this," he said.

"Ruin what?" she said. "You mean this?" She turned her face up to his, closed her eyes and leaned in. Their lips touched lightly but instead of coming together she felt his pull away. When she opened her eyes she found him looking at her, a hint of sadness in his expression.

"You... we... shouldn't," he said. "—Everything is perfect between us just as it is. You are perfect."

"Don't be ridiculous, you just pointed out that I'm a klutz."

"That is just one of your many fine qualities...."

She whacked him on the shoulder and they laughed.

"It's almost dark," she said, as they collected their pails. "We better get going."

When they reached the road they ran up the hill at top speed, careful not to spill any of their precious bounty.

What did he mean? Why shouldn't she kiss him?

CHAPTER 22

D oreen had crushed exactly four cups of berries into a bloody pulp and carefully measured the pectin and sugar knowing that only by striking the perfect balance would the jam set into a pleasing consistency.

She heard Bud strolling into the kitchen from the hallway, felt him take up a position beside her. He picked up the slotted spoon from the roiling pot, brought it to his mouth and licked it.

"Wow! That's hot!"

She gave him an amused look. "It's 220 degrees."

"I thought things boil at 212 degrees," Bud said as his tongue collected the remaining bits of scarlet compote from his lips.

"At sea level water boils at 212 degrees and after that it turns to vapour which is still water but in a different form. Other materials remain liquid at temperatures higher than water. In this case the sugar in the mix makes the jam remain a liquid even though it's over 212 degrees. Don't forget I took chemistry in high school."

"Jam making should come with a warning: Tasting may be hazardous to your lips!" He rubbed his mouth. "Yowzah!"

She felt his hand gentle on the small of her back. Tender. Comforting.

"Doreen, you can take the car this afternoon if you like."

"I picked up groceries this morning. Besides, don't you need it to get gas for the mower?"

"That can wait. The keys are on the hook."

"Thank you, honey." She offered him a light kiss but before she knew it he was sweeping her into his arms and hugging her with his whole being. His arms encircled her shoulders and his mouth was next to her ear.

"Dory. I'm sorry for not being more supportive."

"I love you too," she said, returning his embrace.

✠ ✕ ✠

The next day Doreen looked down at the floor where the linoleum was showing signs of wear and tear. She had given up on her business and along with it her dreams of a second car. The extra money she had earned had been insignificant. What a joke. But the family still needed more money and she was desperate to think of ways she might contribute. She had stopped trying to convince herself that staying at home, looking after her family was enough; it was a lie. It felt as though opening that first Avon kit had released an annoying genie who was constantly hovering over her shoulder, pestering her to make another wish. There had to be something she could do with everything she'd learned. Okay, sister, buck up and think things through. Well, for one thing, no one going door-to-door earns more than pin money. And two, the cost of operating a car and providing wine and cheese at meetings would eat up most of that. Three, no one understands the Avon business model or product line better than her. That's got to amount to something. There's got to be something out there exactly right for her.

CHAPTER 23

Jane opened her bedroom window to let in some air. Doreen had cooked a special meatloaf dinner to celebrate Bud's promotion at work and the kids had been unable to excuse themselves until after the home-made applesauce cake was eaten and all the dishes washed, dried and put away. Now it was almost 8:30 p.m. but the attic room was still stifling. She lay on her side on the bed and gazed over the neighbourhood, scanning for anything interesting and... ha! She sat up and leaned towards the window. What was that? These days Scott usually waited until around 9:30 to start their conversation. This series of dim repetitive flashes was too early.

"R you there"

"R you there"

She picked up her flashlight and the magnifying lens.

"Yes" she responded.

"Meet oak"

"Meet oak"

How strange. What did he mean?

"Tomorrow" she signaled back.

"Tonight"

It was almost dark now and soon it would be completely black in the forest. She didn't relish the thought of sneaking out again, deceiving her parents and being in the woods without her family knowing... But it must be something important, she reasoned, or Scott would have waited until they saw each other the next day. She decided to go.

"Ok," she signaled back, "when"

"Nine"

"Ok"

She picked up her book, opened it to where she had left off and started to read. Suddenly it was almost 9:00. She would be late! She quickly climbed out her window and dropped onto the lawn. She ran past the quiet houses to the forest edge and started down the path. Her flashlight beam leapt ahead as she trotted along to the sound of twigs snapping underfoot.

No reason to worry, she told herself. No reason.

A raccoon sauntered across the path in front of her, its eyes glowing ghoulishly. She jumped back.

Calm down!

She continued along the familiar route, hyper-alert, scanning the environment for anything unexpected. All she could hear was her own breath and the sound of a breeze rustling the tips of the surrounding trees. Eventually, a moonless sky opened up above her but the trail remained shrouded in the blanket of night. As she walked deeper into the forest doubt began to creep in. Why did she need to go all the way to the oak? It was still far ahead… and well off the path… Something didn't seem right.

Then, out of the blackness came a thumping sound. She stopped walking and listened intently. It was coming from up ahead on the path and getting closer. Something large and heavy was coming towards her – fast. Instinctively, she turned off her flashlight and stepped off the path. Moments later heavy footsteps thundered past her and continued along the trail.

Was that Scott? Why was he running? She was about to call his name when the footsteps stopped and a cry of alarm rang out. She froze in place. As she strained to make out what was happening, the throaty growl of a large animal filled the night air. Then came screams of terror and the sound of a scuffle. A terrible fight had broken out.

She backtracked around a bend in the trail and ducked down behind the foliage. The sweet smell of squashed blackberries told her that she was at the base of a briar. She got down on her belly and snaked her way into the underbrush towards the sounds. Thorns ripped her sleeves and scratched her face and neck as she struggled forward. It was no use; the briar was too thick and the night too black for her to see anything. Could she dare to use her flashlight? It was risky but the only way to find out what was happening. She took aim and fired it up. The beam of yellow light slashed through the blackness and illuminated two large figures locked in battle on the path. One was a man and the other a large black animal with gleaming white incisors.

Something seemed familiar. It was Rosie! Rosie was fighting a man on the path! Who was he? She couldn't tell – he was facing away from the light. He was wearing a dark coat and seemed to have dark hair... Rosie had the man's lower leg in his powerful jaws and was tugging forcefully while the man cursed and kicked at the dog with his other leg. The man grabbed Rosie by the scruff and pried his leg free. In a flash the dog spun around, broke the man's grasp and launched another attack. As the man's arms flew up defensively, the dog's jaws clamped down on an exposed wrist. With a roar of pain, the man brought his foot back and delivered a powerful blow to the animal's soft underbelly. Poor Rosie yelped in pain, crashed down on the path and slunk away.

The man stood facing away from her rubbing his wrist. Was it Scott? From her spot on the forest floor it wasn't possible to tell. After a moment he looked around and appeared to notice the light coming from her flashlight. Slowly he began walking towards her, head down, following the illuminated line leading straight to her.

She quickly killed the light, plunging the woods back into complete darkness. The man's footsteps stopped briefly then started up again. She was too terrified to move. She could hear his heavy breathing getting closer. Her heart was pounding so hard she was sure it would give her away.   The crunch of footsteps stopped next to her hiding place.

"Who's there?" said a hoarse voice.

She heard the rustle of movement on the path and sensed the man crouching down and peering into the briar. She tried desperately to press further into the underbrush, but a large cane snagged her chin. Ignoring the pain she pushed against the rows of thorns, feeling a seam open down the front of her neck. It was no use; the briar was too dense for her to go any deeper. All she could do was keep still and pray he would give up looking. She held her breath and listened intently. She thought she detected the stirring of foliage... then she felt something brush up against the side of her shoe. Was it a hand? Instinctively she yanked her legs up towards her belly, making herself as small as possible. A tiny whimper escaped her lips as she faced the truth. There was no way out; her hideaway had become a prison.

"I know you're in there," said the man unhurriedly.

Her options, far too limited, flew through her mind. Screaming would be useless; no one was near enough to hear. Her jaw was clenched and her hands had formed into tight little balls... but there was no way to fight from her position. She had only one choice... she could try to talk her way out. She mustered her courage and did her best to adopt a neutral, non-accusatory tone.

"Who's there?" She asked.

"Who do you th..." The low, raspy voice stopped mid-sentence as a deep rumbling sound arose from nearby. Rosie had come back! The growl started in the lowest registers of the dog's throat and quickly escalated to a loud, guttural snarl. The message was unmistakable, "One false move and I'll tear you apart!"

The man spun on his haunches and let fly with a string of curses. From her hiding place Jane heard the sound of a scuffle and more angry snarls. Then came the rapid thud of footsteps. The man was running... running away down the path. She was safe!

Rosie gave chase for a few yards barking furiously but then stopped and returned to her.

She eased herself backwards, gingerly working her way out of the thorny tunnel. "Here I am, boy! My dear, sweet Rosie!"

The dog leapt into her lap and began licking her face. She clasped him to her and hugged him tightly.

A few minutes later she and Rosie were running frantically up the deserted street. At last she burst through the front door of her house and stood doubled over, gasping for air.

"Mom! Dad!"

Bud and Doreen ran out of the living room and she fell into their arms, crying and shaking.

"What happened?" said Doreen. "Where have you been? You're bleeding!" She took her daughter's head in her hands and lifted it up, revealing a long vertical slash. "Helen!" she called out, "bring me the first aid kit!"

Jane sobbed for several minutes while Doreen dabbed at the jagged tear starting at her chin and running down the side of her neck to her collarbone. After wiping away the blood, she applied pressure to the wound.

Finally, everything tumbled out – the friendship with

Scott, the mirror in the tree, the secret communications, the urgent request to meet and the terrifying events on the path.

"Who was it?" demanded Bud.

She shook her head. "I don't know for certain. It was too dark."

"Was it one of those Mason boys? … Which one?"

"I'm so confused," she whimpered. "I thought Scott and I were friends."

"It's okay, sweetheart. Everything will be all right," said Doreen, gently rocking her.

CHAPTER 24

The sight of Jane's wound and hearing her story was a gut-punch. None of Bud's experience with violence as a police officer had prepared him for seeing his own daughter bloodied. He could feel the muscles of his jaw pulsing rhythmically and his mouth stretching into a scowl. He marched down the hallway and kicked Doreen's Avon kit, sending the contents flying against the door. "Why don't you get rid of that crap? It's been lying there for weeks!"

"BUD! Stop it!" cried Doreen.

"I'm going over there," he said, angrily. "You stay here with the kids."

Jane was huddled on the sofa under her mother's arm. Helen sat wide-eyed at the other end of the chesterfield while Andy peeked out from his bedroom.

Bud yanked on his overcoat and stormed into the night, slamming the door behind him. He was oblivious to the dampness of the cold air, the glare of the single streetlight. By the time he reached the Mason home his fury was beyond containment.

He strode up the gravel driveway and pounded his fist on the heavy front door. After a few moments, he pounded again, harder. Finally, the door opened and George Mason peered out, looking wary.

"What's this about?"

Without answering, Bud kicked the door open wide, sending George reeling backwards.

Regaining his balance, George stood his ground. "Bud, what the hell?"

Bud strode into the entrance hall. "Keep your asshole,

deviant boys away from my daughters.... Or so help me, I will make all of you regret it for the rest of your lives!" He jabbed his finger into George's astonished face.

Margaret appeared from the kitchen doorway. Her colourless hair hung limply beside her face, amplifying her drawn features. Scott ran halfway down the stairs and stopped short when he saw Bud. Jim materialized in the hall, holding a jacket, and took up a spot near a huge wardrobe.

"Bud," said Margaret, her lower lip quivering. "What are you talking about?"

"One of your boys lured my daughter into the woods and tried to attack her," said Bud.

George looked around at Jim. "What do you know about this?" he demanded.

"Nothin'," said Jim. He crossed his arms and leaned against the wardrobe, steely-eyed. "Why don't you ask Scott? He's friends with one of them."

All eyes turned to Scott. He looked stricken and the blood drained from his face. He walked the rest of the way downstairs, and then his legs folded beneath him and he sank to the bottom step, head bowed.

In one stride Bud was towering over him. "Stay away from Jane, *you son-of-a-bitch!*"

Margaret sobbed.

"Cut it out, Margaret!" snapped George. "Get back in the kitchen."

Bud looked down at the boy, so close to his steel-toed boot, gangly arms and legs folded like origami. "Listen, you little shit." He grabbed Scott's shirt and yanked him to his feet. "If you so much as look in my daughter's direction after today, I will come over here and rip your guts out and have what's left of you thrown in jail forever. *Understand?*"

Scott could only blink back tears.

George lurched forward, grabbed Bud's hands and wrested them from Scott's shirt.

"Don't say a word, Scott," he commanded. "Bud, I won't have you barging in here and threatening my family like this. I don't know what happened to your daughter, but both of my boys were here inside with us all evening. You don't have a shred of evidence one of them was involved. Do you!"

Bud fought to regain control of himself, calling upon his training as a peace office, but it was no use. The blood pounding in his head, the putrid smell of fried organ meat coming from the kitchen, and the sight of Jim smirking in the hallway was overwhelming. He leaned into Scott's terrified face.

"I want to know exactly what happened, and you're going to tell me," he scowled.

Scott began to speak, "Mr... Stewart...."

"Quiet Scott!" said George, as he pushed Bud away from his son. "Detective Stewart was just leaving.... And I fully intend to take this incident up with his captain." Then he strode across the hall and flung open the front door.

Before Bud knew it, he was outside, striding down the road, fists jammed into his coat pockets. A cruel rain had started to fall but he marched on, barely noticing. He felt powerless. A failure as a cop. A failure as a husband. A failure as a father. Weak. All he heard was the rhythmic thud of his boots hitting the pavement. He kept walking, not knowing where he was going....

PART THREE

REFLECTION

CHAPTER 25

Jane went to bed hoping the day would finally be over, but it refused her this comfort. It just kept on going. Alone in the darkness, she stared at the ceiling, a carousel of thoughts whirling in her head.

Could that have been Scott? She had trusted him. What might have happened if Rosie had not somehow gotten out and found her? She shivered and pulled her blankets up to her neck, fingers exploring the dressing her mother had applied. Closing her eyes brought back the smell of blackberries and the musky forest floor... and all the terrible sounds. Her eyes flew open again, banishing the memories for the moment, and her mind moved on to her father. She had never seen him so angry. He had been almost unrecognizable. Is this how he acts on his job when he makes arrests in the city? She imagined him in a dark alley, glaring down at a cowering teenager, the marijuana joint dropping from the boy's fingers, his gaping mouth and her father's clenched fist readying to launch a brutal strike. Her hands flew to her face. Where was he? It had been so long since he went over to Scott's house. And what about her mother? She had looked so sad and worried as she went about cleaning up her Avon supplies.

Tears pooled in her eyes until they spilled over and trickled across her temples, into her hair. Slowly she became aware of Sophie hunched beside the pillow and turned her head. The cat began licking away the salty tracks with her sandpaper tongue. Offering reassurance. Don't cry, mistress.

A click announced the door to her room opening, letting in a dim stream of light. A small dark shape entered, followed by a larger one.

"Jane, we could not sleep," said Andy as he crept across the room and onto the end of her bed.

Behind him tiptoed Helen, clasping her dressing gown closed.

Jane pulled Andy up beside her and patted the end of the bed – an invitation for Helen to sit.

Once settled, Andy started to cry softly. "Why is Dad so angry? Did you do something bad? I promise I won't tell. We could tell Dad we're sorry for always making him mad.... Maybe buy him a present?" He looked up at Jane hopefully.

She put her arms around him. "It's not you, Andy. You did nothing wrong. You are a sweet, sweet boy." She thought for a moment. "It's my fault. I went into the woods against the rules. That's why Dad is so upset."

Helen put up her hand. "It's not your fault either. Someone tricked you. You were... lured," she said, savouring the word.

"I don't understand," said Jane. "It must have been Scott. He's the only one who knows our code. But we're supposed to be friends."

"Boys do not make very good friends," said Helen sadly. "I should have warned you." Her head dropped and her pretty mouth turned down at the edges. "Bobby has been telling people that I... you know... went all the way with him. But I swear I didn't. I let him kiss me and... maybe a little more than that... but that's all."

"Oh, Helen."

Heavy footsteps could be heard clomping up the stairs and the children fell silent.

Bud's huge frame filled the doorway. "What's going on in here?" he demanded, flicking on the light.

Andy whimpered and both girls shrank back.

Bud stepped into the room, water dripping from his

drenched coat. "Andy and Helen, go back down to your bedrooms, now," he said. "All of you, go to sleep. We will talk about this in the morning."

He stepped aside as the two children obediently filed by, then he turned off the light without another word.

Jane listened to him walking slowly down the stairs.

❉ ✄ ❉

Doreen was waiting at the bottom of the stairs. With every step down, Bud felt more deflated.

"My own children are afraid of me," he said, when he reached the ground floor.

He opened the front door, stepped into the night and sat on the stoop. Not even Rosie followed him out. He pulled his smokes from the pocket of his coat. Cigarette in mouth, he struck a match. The rain-drenched tip flared briefly then went out.

CHAPTER 26

The lawns had gone from green to yellow and now they were a parched white, bleached by the late summer sun. Doreen washed and dried the dinner dishes and then went to find Bud who was outside watering his struggling vegetable garden. Only the radishes had thrived, the other plants having succumbed under his sporadic attention. She put her arms around him and squeezed a hug from him.

"Bud, there has been so much tension around this house lately that I can hardly breathe. We all need a break. Maybe we should go on holiday. You know, do something fun with the kids."

Bud started to shake his head. "We can't afford a fancy trip."

"It doesn't have to be expensive. Why don't we just pack the tent and go camping for a few days before school starts? We can stay for next to nothing at the campsites in Washington and Oregon and the food is so much cheaper down there. The kids can go swimming and hiking and build campfires. Come on, Bud, it will be a good break before the summer is gone. What do you think? Remember the fun we had camping on our honeymoon?"

A reluctant grin pulled up the corners of his mouth. "Yeah, sleeping under the stars and not even noticing the rain clouds coming in. Just when we thought we had moved beyond the back seats of cars, there we were again!" He laughed. "You're right – we need a change of scenery. Let's surprise the kids and go away. I still have a few days of holiday left."

�֍ ✗ �֍

Doreen packed the trunk of the car like a jigsaw puzzle using a checklist to make sure she included all the required camping gear: sleeping bags, pillows, food, dishes, stove, fuel, utensils, towels, and clothes. And then they were off, crossing all the bridges it took to get out of Vancouver. In the back seat Helen was seething. They were ruining her summer by taking her away from her friends. And Jane on the other side of the seat looked sullen too, staring out the window. Only Andy, squished into the middle with pillows on either side to buffer him from his two moody sisters, seemed excited. But he was holding it in for fear of being elbowed. Rosie sat on the front bench seat between Bud and Doreen who held a plastic bowl in case he got car-sick again.

The family headed south along Highway 99 stopping at the Peace Arch border crossing where the customs officer asked a few basic questions and then waved them into Washington. When the kids and the dog got restless, Bud pulled into a gas station south of Bellingham for a pit stop. He felt his shoulders soften slightly as he filled up the car with cheap US gas and watched Jane lead Rosie into the trees for a pee. Helen had run into the store and came out with the latest *Seventeen* magazine. As she jumped in the back seat with her magazine clutched to her chest, he gave her a disapproving glance.

"Dad, don't bug me," she said. "I bought this with my babysitting money. Besides, it's the newest one – not yet available in Canada." She slumped down and started to flip through the pages, happy for the moment.

They sped along in silence with Doreen trying to read the unwieldy roadmap on her lap at the same time as the road signs whipped by. Bud flipped on the radio and tried to tune in a local station. "Nothing but static," he said, giving up and lighting a cigarette.

Doreen looked at him with a frown. "Bud, please don't smoke in the car or at least roll down the window."

He pretended to ignore her but after a few moments he rolled down his window halfway and flicked out the burning cigarette. "I was going to do that anyway," he said, a faint smile creeping across his face.

"I know you were, dear," said Doreen, smiling back.

"Let's play *I spy*!" Andy yelled.

His sisters just ignored him.

Defeated, he sank into his seat between the girls. "This is going to be the worst vacation ever."

A couple hours later Doreen spotted the turnoff sign to the campsite where they planned to spend the first night. "It's the next turn off, Bud."

"Too late. We're in the wrong lane. Dammit," Bud cursed as the car flew by the exit.

"It's okay, Bud, we can find a spot to turn around and go back."

They drove on for many miles – there seemed to be no exits on Interstate 5.

"At this rate, we'll be in Mexico soon," groused Bud.

Just then a sign popped up on the right with the welcome words, *"Mossy Hollows Campsite Next Exit."*

"I think we should try this one," said Doreen. "It's not on the map but everyone is tired and it's getting late."

It was nearly dark when Bud pulled into the campsite. He was relieved to see available spots for tenting. He drove around and chose the prettiest, most private spot and pulled in. Rosie leapt out as soon as the door opened and promptly puked. The kids helped to unload the car, hauling the tent and sleeping bags from the bottom of the trunk. The campsite was quiet with only a few other campers visible. They hurriedly set up the canvas tent, pounding the last pegs into the copper-brown soil just as darkness fully arrived. By the time Doreen had heated up the canned stew on the camp stove the stars were out in full force.

Andy looked up in awe. "Dad, how come there are so many more stars here than in Canada?"

Bud smiled and explained that they were far from the lights of the city which made them easier to see. Before bed they all trudged to the pit toilets and held their breath.

A crack of thunder announced an oncoming storm. Doreen got the children settled into their sleeping bags. "Now remember not to touch the sides of the tent or the water will seep through."

❈ ✕ ❈

Jane shivered in her flannel-lined sleeping bag and pulled it over her head. As she listened to the splatter of the raindrops overhead and crash of distant thunder her thoughts returned to the episode in the woods. Neither of the Mason boys had been seen around the neighbourhood since it happened, which suited her just fine. She was dreading the inevitable moment when she would run into them at school.

Eventually the storm passed and silence blanketed the campsite as the exhausted travellers dropped off to sleep.

In the middle of the night a barrage of images exploded in Jane's head – flashes of light, a violent struggle, razor-sharp teeth, angry snarls and anguished cries…. Her hands flew up to her ears but the terrifying sounds continued.

"NO! NO!"

❈ ✕ ❈

Bud was jolted awake. He strained to see through the dark but couldn't make anything out. Then he heard Helen comforting Jane who was sobbing quietly. He patted Doreen's arm. "I'll go," he whispered, and he crawled over to the girls and kneeled at the end of their sleeping bags.

"Jane, Helen, I'm here... and I'm always going to be here... for both of you... and Andy. Nothing bad is ever going to happen as long as I'm around. Do you believe me?"

Dimly he saw their heads slowly bobbing in unison.

"Yes, Dad." And with that the girls scrambled out of their sleeping bags and down to Bud and he caught them up in his girder-strong arms. He was so filled with love his heart would surely burst.

※ ✕ ※

Doreen fried bacon and scrambled some eggs for breakfast and then they all pitched in to pack up the car and head out to their next destination. Driving south down the windy coastal road the panoramic views of the Pacific Ocean were stunning. After they crossed the border into Oregon magnificent dunes appeared.

"Wow! What planet are we on now?" Andy shouted as he tried to climb into the front seat for a better view.

"Oh, I read about these in the brochure I picked up at the gas station." Doreen said. "They are so beautiful! Just look at the expanse of windswept sand. Look how high the dunes are!"

Bud pulled the car into a viewpoint and Doreen jumped out and took pictures of the breathtaking scene.

A short time later they were cruising into the Pacific Sands Resort.

"Bud," said Doreen, "Look at this place! Real flush toilets, hot showers, a volleyball court and wow, it's fantastic, isn't it? I know it's a bit more expensive but let's splurge!"

Bud didn't need convincing to spend the extra ten dollars. He'd pay that and more any day to see his wife this happy. He stepped lightly into the front office to book their spot while the kids helped unload the car then changed into their bathing suits and ran off to explore the dunes. After setting up the camp he and Doreen enjoyed a barefoot walk along the beach, the salty water tickling their toes. How long had it been since he'd held his wife's hand? And she looked so playful and young... more beautiful than the Pacific Ocean.

❊ ✕ ❊

Gross! Helen undressed and entered the tiny shower stall intent on not allowing any part of her flesh to touch the walls. As the warm water ran over her shoulders and down her back, her mood improved. Maybe the boy with the wavy blond hair and Puka shell necklace she had met on the beach that afternoon would be there. That would make this so-called vacation a little more tolerable. Good thing I brought along my new white dress – he'll be sure to notice me. Oh, and my choker necklace... can't forget that....

Doreen eyed her disapprovingly when she joined the family at the picnic table and slid warily along the rough-hewn bench seat. Mustn't snag the gauzy material or worse, get slivers!

"You look very pretty, Helen, but we're not going to visit the queen! We're going to a bonfire on the beach."

Everyone laughed.

Helen rolled her eyes. What did she care about their lame opinions anyway.

After their meal the family walked to the beach to join other families perched on logs surrounding a large fire built on the sand. The wood was burning hot and sparks flew in lazy swirls up into an indigo sky. The sweet sound of a guitar serenaded the group and drew her attention. No way! It was her new blond friend, sitting across from her. When he started to sing she instantly fell under his spell... his voice ...the music he plucked from the strings of his guitar... the light from the campfire twinkling in his eyes....

Bobby who? What a jerk he had turned out to be. She smiled to herself. This boy was so much cuter, and talented!

"Darn these mosquitoes!" said Bud, slapping himself furiously. "They're eating me alive!"

"Me, too," said Jane, swatting the back of her neck.

"Yeah," said Andy, waving his arms around. "They're spoiling all the fun."

"That's odd," Doreen said. "They're not bothering me and normally they love me."

"I don't know what you're talking about," said Helen. "No bugs around me." But when she looked around she saw it was true. Even the guitar player had to interrupt his songs to swat away the pesky mozzies.

"Hummm," Doreen said as she picked up the sample tube of Skin So Soft that she and Helen had been using to moisturize. "I wonder if this stuff...."

"I'm outa here," said Bud, interrupting her train of thought. "Come, Rosie. Come, Andy.... Honey?"

"Okay, I'm coming. But next time you should all try my lotion."

The song ended and Doreen hustled Jane and Andy away

from the warmth of the campfire and the buzz of the insects back toward the tent.

"Don't stay out too late, Helen, or I'll come and find you," warned Bud.

❋ ✕ ❋

Bud was pleased to see the family members enjoying themselves. Even Jane was doing better.

He squeezed Doreen's hand on the path back to their campsite. "You did good, Dory, suggesting this trip."

"Yeah, Mom," says Andy. "You did good."

"Well, I did *well*," says Doreen. "Or you could say: 'You did a good thing.' Do you see the difference, Andy?"

"Really?" Jane says, shooting Andy a sympathetic look. "Grammar lesson right now?"

❋ ✕ ❋

Bud was tucked into his bag but still wide awake when Helen crawled into the tent, singing one of the folk songs that kid had been playing. Blowin' in the effing wind? What's that supposed to mean? And what could that self-absorbed twerp possibly know about life? He's not even out of high school.... Let it go.

❋ ✕ ❋

The next morning the family packed up for the long drive home. As they crossed the border back into Washington, Bud started singing – his throaty baritone filling the car's confined quarters. There was no escaping it. Now this is what a real folk song sounds like.

I've been workin' on the railroad
All the live-long day
I've been workin' on the railroad...

One by one his family took up the song and Rosie howled and eventually even Helen joined in the chorus.

In the driveway, the doors to the Chevy sprung open and disgorged the family, tired but happy. Helen ran into the house demanding first rights to the phone while Andy headed into the kitchen for a snack. Jane went to check on Sophie and see if anything was left of the extra-large bowl of Friskers chow Doreen had put out for when the family was away. Unimpressed, the cat turned her back and walked away. Bud and Doreen started the exhausting task of unpacking the funky-smelling camping gear and sorting through the piles of sand-laden laundry. Overall, the trip had been worth all the work.

Chapter 27

With September came gusts of wind and shorter days but temperatures remained warm. The sisters spent Labour Day long weekend preparing for back to school; sifting through their closets for items that could still be worn and tossing out those that could not – Helen's pile of rejects being considerable higher than Jane's. Each girl had been allowed to buy a few new pieces and Helen had tried to instruct Jane on how the new should co-ordinate with the old but her guidance fell on deaf ears. Everything went with blue jeans, which were the staple of Jane's wardrobe, even though they couldn't be worn at school. And she couldn't have cared less anyway.

The first day of school arrived and Jane and Andy left the house together. Andy at once ran off to join his friends heading to the elementary school and she was left on her own. So many things were on her mind. What would her grade nine schedule be like? What teachers would she get? But most of all, how will she react when she sees Scott, or Jim? They could hardly be avoided in such a small school. At least they were in a higher grade, so maybe the inevitable could be postponed for a few days... maybe.

She breathed in deeply, knowing this was soil-infused air, the byproduct of the previous night's rain. As she squelched through the mushy-cornflake leaves on the side of the road, she looked up and saw Clara at the end of her driveway, waving furiously.

She waved back and picked up her gait. The two girls embraced.

"I've missed you," said Clara.

"Me you too!" replied Jane smiling. "Good summer?"

"Hellish! The black flies were the size of helicopters so you couldn't go outside, and my grandparents just wanted to play gin rummy all day. And oh my lord, if I have to watch any more of that schmoozer, Merv Griffin, I'll shoot myself. You would have gone mad."

Jane laughed. "How about after you got home? Didn't you hang out with your other friends?"

"They were soooo boring," said Clara. "All they ever wanted to do was watch TV or go to the mall."

Soon they were in step, walking the familiar route to the high school and talking a mile and minute.

"Look what I got," said Jane. "My mom said it was time, like it or not." She pulled her T-shirt off one shoulder revealing a quarter-inch wide white strap.

"Oh my god! I guess pigs can fly!" laughed Clara.

"It's so binding!" said Jane. "I feel like I've been put in a straitjacket."

"Well, look on the bright side, you won't have to change for PE facing the wall anymore."

"You noticed?"

"Are you kidding, everyone noticed."

Jane stopped in her tracks but then started laughing. "Jeez, what else haven't you told me?" she said, knuckling her friend in the bicep.

"Ow! That's a conversation for another day," said Clara. "What's that red mark on your neck?"

"Oh… uh… it's from a blackberry-picking accident."

HONK!

The girls turned to see a brightly painted VW van covered in PEACE and END THE WAR bumper stickers roll up across from the school. The passenger side door swung open and a pair of long legs poked out clad in platform shoes.

"Oh my god, is that Helen?" asked Clara.

"Yup, uh-huh," Jane stammered as she watched the latest iteration of her sister emerge from the van. She was sporting a micro-mini shift dress in a tie-dyed print of pink, green and purple and her face was largely obscured by oversized sunglasses despite the cloudy sky. Her hair was parted in the middle and tucked behind ears adorned with hooped earrings. The van radio blared Country Joe counting and chanting about death and the driver leaned out the passenger door and called after her, "Pick you up later, Babe!"

Jane watched her sister sashay across the road onto the school grounds then sized up the long-haired, bearded man. It was the first time she had seen him close up. He looked old, at least twenty, and grubby.

"She just met that guy last week and now she's hanging out with him all the time," she said. "He's living out of his van in Cate's Park. Helen says he's a conscientious objector, but my dad calls him a draft dodger. He's going to be picking her up and driving her to school in the morning so she can sleep in, if you can believe it. My parents are going insane...."

"Won't she get in trouble for wearing that outfit to school?"

"Who knows and who cares!" replied Jane as they dashed up the school stairs just as the bell rang.

The morning moved slowly through the usual administrative tasks – attendance, class assignments and the handing out of lists of supplies for parents to buy. At lunch, Clara was waiting for Jane in the hall. Their lockers were in the same area and after checking that their combination locks were working, they went outside and sat on the grass to eat. Jane was munching hungrily on her baloney sandwich and listening to Clara whine about her class schedule and teachers when she felt another set of eyes upon her. She squinted into the sun and saw Scott standing in the filtered light beneath the maple tree that grew beside the school entranceway. She felt her pulse quicken and her temperature spike. She immediately looked back at Clara.

Clara stopped mid-sentence and stared at her. "You look like you've just seen a ghost."

Jane motioned with her head towards Scott. "Look over there and tell me what you see."

"I see nothing but a bunch of plants."

Jane looked back at the maple. Scott was gone. She scanned the schoolyard, but he was nowhere to be seen.

"What's going on?" asked Clara.

Jane started to speak in measured tones but almost instantly the dam burst and words gushed out of her. By the time she had finished Clara knew all about her friendship with Scott and the events of late summer, including the terrifying night in the forest.

"When you told me this morning that big scratch was from a blackberry bush, I didn't buy it. Now it makes sense," said Clara.

"I'm sorry. The whole thing was so scary I still have trouble talking about it, even with my mom."

Clara nodded. "And I wasn't exactly available to you. What a lousy friend I turned out to be."

"Don't say that. Just think of all those crazy adventures I dragged you into. You got in trouble with your mom so many times because of me. I trust you more than anyone."

"Me you too." Clara hugged her again. "So, was it Scott in the woods that night?"

"I don't know. I can't believe it was him. He's so gentle and sweet. I thought we had something... I don't know... special."

"I told you he liked you… sounds like you like him back?" Clara's voice was a little shaky.

"No, I mean, yes, but not anymore."

Clara looked down at the ground and was silent. Eventually she asked, "Did you kiss?"

"No… but I wanted to."

The school bell jangled and Jane jumped to her feet. After a few steps she noticed her friend was still sitting on the grass, head slumped, not making any attempt to stand.

"Come on," she said. She ran back, took Clara's hand and pulled her up. "We don't want to be late for Mr. Klassen's Socials class."

�֍ ✕ ✖

"Welcome, class." Mr. Klassen, wearing his usual tweed blazer and horn-rimmed glasses, smiled from the front of the class-room. "I trust everyone enjoyed their long summer break with no lectures to listen to and no pesky homework assignments to worry about."

Everyone smiled back and nodded.

"Well, now we are going to get your young minds thinking again. Let's get those wheels turning. This term we are going to study 20th Century history and the wars that have shaped modern Europe, Asia and North America." A few groans en-sued but a couple of the boys perked up. "Let's start today's discussion with the Vietnam War, something you are all fa-miliar with. How many of you have seen the nightly newscasts on TV about this war?"

A sea of hands went up.

"Can anyone tell us why the United States decided to enter the war a couple of years ago?"

One of the boys in the back row put up his hand, "Because they want our side to win?"

"Yes, that's part of it. Anyone else?"

Tony raised his hand. "Because they don't want the communists to take over."

"Very good," said Mr. Klassen. "Who knows what a communist is?"

Clara piped up, "My dad says it's someone who wants to take away everyone's property and force them to work for nothing... and if you don't agree you get put in a work camp or killed."

"Hum," said the teacher. "But why would people fight on the side of communism if it's so bad? Does that system of government have anything to offer that people might want?"

Tony chimed in again, "The communists promise to take money from the rich people and give it to the poor people. All the poor people like that idea."

Mr. Klassen nodded. "So there are two sides to the story?"

Clara put up her hand again. "My dad says the leaders just take all the money for themselves. And that people who don't get to own their own stuff won't work hard. So the system doesn't work."

"Clara, these are interesting points. Now, I want you to all think about how it would feel to be asked by your country to go and fight in this war."

The class fell silent, the boys looked especially uncomfortable.

"What does it take to get young men, many of them not much older than you, to go overseas to a foreign country to kill and possibly be killed?"

Jane looked around at her male classmates. Some shifted in their seats. Tony, the Mason boys, the whole boys' basketball team – if they lived in America could be called up in only a few years and sent to war. It seemed absurd. Incredibly cruel and... terrifying. She suddenly felt sympathy for Helen's American friend. "The government could try to make them really believe in the cause, like during WWII," she said. "But in this case, a lot don't believe in the war and so their government is drafting them and forcing them to go."

"Excellent insights, Jane. Now, everyone, take out your notebooks and write a short essay on how you feel about the war. It's not for marks; it's just an exercise to get you thinking."

The classroom filled with the rustle of opening notebooks. Jane stared at the blank first page. What about Scott? They had never talked about the war. He seemed so gentle and kind, the moment they almost kissed had been so tender. She closed her eyes and felt the nearness of his lips again. Was he capable of hurting others... of hurting her? She picked up her pen and started to write.

The rest of the day flew by and she was amazed when the bell rang to signal the end of classes. She pushed through students grabbing books and spilling out into the hall, eager to pick up her gym strip and get to the basketball team tryouts. Jim Mason and Bobby Lesson were roughhousing by their lockers so she steered a wide path around them but could feel both sets of eyes on her.

In the girls' changing room, she and Clara pulled on their blue shorts and white T-shirts.

"I hope we make the team," Jane said. "My dad was point guard on his high school team and he's been spending Saturday mornings shooting hoops with me here at school." She sighed. "I don't think I have his talent."

A dozen girls waited in the bleachers until the boys finished

up and then headed onto the gym floor. Jim Mason in his basketball jersey strutted directly toward Jane. She stood her
ground as he brushed by, clipping her shoulder.

"Asshole," she called after him.

"Yup," he replied, looking over his shoulder.

What was that expression on his face?

Energized after tryouts concluded, she and Clara started
for home.

"Jane, I'm certain you'll be picked. You sank more baskets
than anyone else. Plus, you've grown so much; you're the tall-
est girl in our grade now."

"It won't be much fun if you're not on the team. Fingers
crossed for when the postings come out.

"I'm not holding my breath. I'm five-foot-nothing. If I don't
make it, I'll root for you from the sidelines – just don't expect
me to join the cheerleaders. *We give our ass a wiggle! And
make our boobies jiggle!*"

Jane laughed and joined in: *"Then we whirl, whirl, whirl,
until we hurl, hurl, hurl!"*

�❊ ✄ ❊

On autopilot, Doreen moved from the fridge to the cupboard,
checking supplies, planning the week's lunch boxes. Tomorrow
would be tuna sandwiches, apples and homemade rice-crispy
squares. She was starting a new school year along with the
kids. Now that they were back in the classroom, she couldn't
wait to tackle her new project. If things went as planned, her
earlier Avon profits would look like pocket change. She smiled
to herself. It was as if some inner force had sabred off the cork
that she had stuck into her creativity after the kids arrived

and now ideas were bubbling up and gushing out everywhere. She could hardly remember a time when she had felt this energized.

She turned up the radio, got her motor runnin' and grooved along to the beat of Steppenwolf. *Born to be wild... Born to be wild!*

⚔ ✖ ⚔

Walking home after basketball practice, running through her stop-and-start drills, Jane noticed a figure up ahead. It was Scott. He was standing on the side of the road and appeared to be waiting for her. She started to cross the street to avoid him then changed her mind and walked right up to him.

"Was it you?"

He took a step towards her. "I... I...." As he struggled to find words he extended his arms towards her, palms up as if to show he meant no harm. With the movement, the sleeves of his shirt rode up exposing his wrists. On one arm his pale skin was mutilated by angry pink gashes.

Shockwaves coursed through her body. "Stop where you are!" she commanded.

Scott looked confused then glanced down to his exposed arm. "Wait... it wasn't.... It's not what you think."

"Get away from me!" she exclaimed, backing up.

"Wait," he pleaded.

Just then the hippy van, belching black exhaust, came chugging up the road towards them with Helen riding shotgun. Jane flagged it down and the vehicle slowed just enough for her to open the sliding side door and dive in.

"Keep driving," she exclaimed, as she crawled across the

makeshift bed and looked out the back window at Scott's receding figure, the image of the scarred wrist seared into her mind's eye.

CHAPTER 28

The middle of September brought another warm spell. On a Saturday afternoon, Bud called out, "Kids! Go get Rosie and grab your bathing suits. We're celebrating Jane's birthday with a seaside picnic!"

After parking at Ambleside Beach, he raced across the sand and plunged into the bracing water with Rosie galloping in after him. Churning up the spray, he tried to cajole the others into joining them.

Jane played the tease. She ran into the water ankle-deep then quickly leapt back up the beach. Helen made it perfectly clear that she had no intention of getting her new, halter-top bikini wet. Finally, his brave son waded out, unable to resist his father's beckoning arms.

"Attaboy, Andy!"

He waved to Doreen but she had already spread some blankets and a plastic red-and-white checked tablecloth on the sand and was now unpacking potato salad, cold chicken and homemade pickles.

After enjoying the picnic, the family sat on a log silvered by salt and sea spray and watched as the sun, a glowing ember, set the horizon ablaze before dousing itself in Georgia Straight. Bud gave Jane's ponytail a playful tug. "Happy birthday, Janie, I mean Jane. I'm so proud you made the basketball team. You are going to run circles around those other girls. I'll help you practise but I'm no spring chicken... you'll need to let me win once in a while."

"Dad," said Jane, "you can't get away with that senior citizen act with me, you're not even forty."

Bud laughed. "Doreen, pass me that lotion you and Helen

have been using, the bugs are coming for me." She passed him the container and he emptied it into his palm then smeared it on the back of his neck and arms. "Is there any more?"

"Nope, that's the last of the samples."

"You smell like a flower shop," said Jane waving her hand across her nose.

"It's lilac to be exact. And I happen to like the smell. Plus, it's got a nice texture and it's not sticky. Not to mention, it works like a hot damn at keeping the mozzies off."

Doreen cleared her throat. "Bud, I've been thinking... since you like the lotion maybe the other boys at the precinct would also like it. I could order a case and you could hand them out on a trial basis."

Bud stopped rubbing in the cream and looked at his wife; her eyes were brimming with hope and something else was there too. Fear?

"What? How long you been thinking about this?"

"Just since I noticed you seemed to like it. I thought if you like it maybe other men would too. I added a little DEET to it... to make it more potent as a repellent. And the market is potentially huge. Like, maybe the entire City Works department would be interested. I could maybe get the wholesale rights and it wouldn't involve going door-to-door anymore." Doreen's hands, fingers entwined, were pressed against her mouth.

"Honey," he said, shaking his head. "The guys at the precinct don't like girlie stuff."

All the kids fell silent; the only sound was the lapping of waves and the outrage of a distant gull.

Finally, Bud continued. "But if there is anyone who can sell perfumed lotions to men, it's you. Why not give it a try?"

He gave her a big smile and was almost bowled over when she launched herself at his neck.

"Thank you, Bud! Your support means everything to me! And I have many, many more ideas! About other products for men and of course for women too! Lotions and skin creams can be mediums for delivery of all kinds of things, even medicine, and the cosmetics industry is completely missing the boat by focusing solely on beauty and fragrance."

"Settle down now," said Bud, still discombobulated by his wife's caress. "We can talk more later. Okay, kids," he called, "now we're going to top off this perfect day with a trip to Pete's Ice Cream Parlor."

"Yay!" chimed all three.

They piled happily into the hot car and drove off, Rosie's head lolling out the window, facing forward, ears flapping in the wind.

Only as Bud pulled into the driveway did the reality of his commitment sink in. Jeez, how am I going to break this lotion thing to the captain?

❀ ✄ ❀

Jane and Helen found themselves alone in the kitchen putting away the picnic leftovers.

"Helen, why are you hanging out with that creepy guy? He looks old enough to be in college, and you've only just started grade eleven."

"Stop being such a nosy brat. He was going to Washington State University but for now he's staying in Canada. He's a kind of exchange student."

"Ya right. What kind of exchange? Selling drugs?"

"Shut up! What do you know about any of that?"

"I can smell it on you. You better pray Dad doesn't. Besides, I thought after that business with Bobby you would steer clear of boys for a while."

Helen lifted the sleeve of her sweater to her face and sniffed it. "Bobby was such a child. So immature! One good thing, though, he finally stopped spreading those awful rumours about me."

"Well, that's good news," said Jane. "But this new guy... you don't really like him, do you?"

"What do you know about love, you just turned thirteen. I'm sixteen now and know what's real and what's not."

"Did you just say *love*?" asked Jane, incredulously.

Helen shot her a scathing look then stomped into her bedroom and slammed the door.

Jane scooped up Sophie from the bottom step, carried her up to her room and deposited her on the bed before flopping down herself. How old did you have to be to fall in love? And what did it feel like? Her mind moved to Scott, as it so often did when she was alone. She rolled onto her side and looked out the window towards the forest. There would be no flashes of light. After the incident in the woods, her father had attacked the oak tree with an axe and smashed the mirror into a thousand shards.

As she lay in the dark she felt an emptiness in her belly, as if she had been hollowed out leaving only her shell behind. Evenings, once the best part of her day, were now flat and featureless. How she missed those nighttime conversations and the unique intimacy they represented – the intriguing new feelings they had stirred within her. She also recalled the many afternoons she and Scott had spent together. They had been effortless and exciting in a way that was different from her time with Clara. He had made her feel appreciated, even admired, despite her tomboyish ways. She had felt optimistic and buoyant... as if anything in life was possible... and the moment they parted she had found herself looking forward to their next meeting. Now all those positive feelings were gone, replaced by a deep sense of loss. And questions. She let out a sigh. What if it wasn't him that night? Why had she not given him a chance to speak, that day on the street? Where would they be now, if she had let him explain?

She rolled onto her other side, away from the window, and begged for sleep to come.

Chapter 29

Doreen sat at the kitchen table, laser focused. Calm. Laid out in front of her were two dozen plastic containers of various shapes and sizes. She picked up a small bottle, removed its cap and set it down. Then she scooped two tablespoons of thick lotion from a bowl, each time levelling off the top with the back of a knife before depositing the substance into the open bottle. She reached for a small glass vessel and, using an eye dropper, drew out a tiny amount of liquid. One, two, three, she counted as the liquid plopped into the bottle. After snapping on the cap, she shook up the mixture, held it up to the light, then reopened it. She applied a small amount to her left forearm and rubbed it in with her fingertip. Then she raised her wrist to her nose and inhaled. Not bad.

She picked up her pen and made a note in a lined notebook which had been carefully divided into columns headed: Base, Additive, Fragrance, Cost per Unit, Proposed Application, Target Market.

On the counter behind her were cartons filled with dozens of similar containers, their lids carefully labelled and colour coded.

❈ ✕ ❈

A swirl of crimson maple leaves accompanied Bud through the front door but he took no notice as he flung his car keys onto the hall table

"Is that you, hon?" called Doreen from the kitchen. "You said you'd be late but this is later than usual. I hope you'll get paid overtime. They're always taking advantage of you now that you're a detective."

He found her peeling carrots into the sink. When she turned to give him a light peck he drew her to him, holding her tight. After a moment he released her, grabbed a beer from the fridge, popped the tab and began sucking it back. Doreen removed her apron, walked into the backyard and sat down on a deckchair. He looked through the window at her, then followed and sat in the chair beside her. On days like this, she could always be depended on to give him time.

"Shitty day," he said, taking a chug from the can.

"I figured."

"Really, really, shitty."

"Yeah?"

"George Mason is down at the station."

"What for?"

"He assaulted his family."

"What? Oh no! Is everyone okay?"

"Margaret's at the station right now and will be taken to a women's shelter later," he replied.

"Is she hurt?"

"Seems to be okay physically, but she's not coping emotionally."

"What about the boys?"

Bud took another swig. "It's bad. Jim's in the hospital... in serious condition. And we don't know where Scott is. We have an officer staked out at the house for when he comes back."

"What happened?"

"We don't have all the details. Looks like George attacked Jim, and Scott must have run off."

"This is terrible," said Doreen. "I saw Margaret a couple months ago when I dropped by to see if she was enjoying her

Avon order. She answered the door wearing her housecoat. She was polite and asked me about my work but she looked exhausted and didn't invite me inside. What will happen to Scott when they find him?"

"He's a minor so he'll be turned over to relatives if they have any and if not, to social services – at least until his mother can take him."

"I can't believe George has it in him to do such a thing." Doreen shook her head. "He seemed so nice when I was over there."

"This isn't the first time that we've been called to the house," Bud said. "The other incidents were minor but who knows what doesn't get reported. That's why I lost my mind after what happened to Jane. I should have stopped her from having anything to do with that family. I shudder to think…."

Doreen leaned over and rubbed the back of his neck. "Jane's fine… nothing really terrible happened."

Bud shook his head slowly and looked down at the ground. "How could a man do that to his family?"

❖ ✕ ❖

Jane stood still in the kitchen peering through the partially open door at her parents. She'd heard everything, seen their grim faces. At Bud's last words, she launched herself away from the doorway, ran up the stairs to her room and flung herself on the bed. She'd always known that the Mason family was different from her own, but she had never imagined something like this. Her father said that Jim was in serious condition… but how serious? And where was Scott? She had to find him. She had to know he was okay.

How could she reach him? Their old signalling system had

been destroyed and besides, Scott would have to be in his room to receive a signal, and it was clear he was avoiding his house. She would have to find him another way. Where would she go if she wanted to hide?

The trails, of course.

CHAPTER 30

After what seemed like an eternity, Jane said good night, crept upstairs and closed her bedroom door. Within moments she was heading down the street, avoiding the halo of the single streetlight. A light fog had settled over the neighbourhood, softening the edges of the houses and trees, making everything look out of focus. The moan of the foghorn in Burrard Inlet accompanied her footsteps as she hurried along.

The mouth of the trail yawned before her, an inky portal, daring her to enter. She stopped in her tracks. What was she doing? This was crazy. Her instincts told her to turn back but her overwhelming desire to see Scott was stronger. Jim was in hospital and Mr. Mason was locked up. Scott would never hurt her, would he? She would be safe. Slowly she inserted her fingers into the pocket of her jacket and drew out her dad's flashlight. It felt heavy and cold in her hand as she directed it down the path and slid the metal button forward. A beam of yellow light flooded the tree-shrouded trail, piercing the darkness, illuminating the way. You've come this far... you can do it. But her feet were rooted to the ground; she could not make herself enter. Memories of that terrible evening, the smell of the forest floor, the physical pain of the thorns tearing her flesh were all too fresh. It would be madness to proceed. But what was she to do now? Then it came to her. Slowly, she raised and lowered her arm, assessing how far the beam reached into the woods. She turned the flashlight off. Two seconds later she turned it on again. Then off, then on. Then she started her message:

Short long long long / Short long / Long short / Short

Again and again she sent the signal into the woods. It

seemed futile. Was Scott even in the forest? But she continued with her four-letter message.

J A N E

J A N E

J A N E.

There was no response. What did she expect? It was a crazy idea in the first place. Her fingers were stiff and achy and her whole body was cold. She turned off the light, tucked it back into her pocket and was about to turn towards home when she caught sight of the outline of a human figure on the leaf-strewn path.

Scott emerged from the shadows. He was grim-faced and dishevelled; dark circles underscored his eyes. "At first I thought it was the police," he said. "I should have known you'd be the one to find me."

"I knew where to look."

"Are you going to turn me in?"

"No, and nobody knows I'm here. Are you alright?"

"I'm okay." After a pause he continued. "Where's my dad?"

"In jail."

He nodded. "What about my mother?"

"The police took her to the station and then a safe house."

"And Jim?"

"He's in Lions Gate Hospital. It sounds like he's really hurt bad."

"Is he going to be okay?" Scott's face was contorted with pain and grief.

"I don't know," she replied. "But he is being looked after and so is your mom."

Scott shoved his hands into his pockets and drew in his shoulders. He dropped his head and looked down, breathing slowly. She watched and waited, not knowing what to do.

Finally, he raised his head. "I have to see him."

"Jim?"

He didn't answer.

"You can't," said Jane. "The police are looking for you. If you go home, they will apprehend you and the same thing will happen if you go to the hospital."

Scott nodded glumly; his gaze still averted. "Is that what you heard?" he asked.

"Yes, my dad said that you can't keep living with your dad and your mom has to go away for a while to get better. I heard them talking about whether you had any relatives that could take you in."

"We don't," said Scott.

"Then they are going to send you to a foster home, at least until your mother is better."

"I'm going to run away," he said. "But I won't leave without seeing Jim."

"Why?"

"You don't understand. No one does." He turned his back on her and took a few steps into the woods.

"I really don't think you should try," said Jane following him. "You'll get caught and he has always been so mean to you anyway, I don't know why you'd risk it."

He turned around and faced her. "Jim is the best friend I have ever had," he said.

"What? He's a jerk. He's been a bully all his life. He's mean…. He makes everyone at school miserable. He pushes you around and makes fun of you. He's a total asshole!"

Scott shot an angry look at her. "Shut up! You don't know anything!" The veins on his neck began to pulse and his fists were clenched. His eyes blazed.

She recoiled in shock. A bolt of fear struck her. She became instantly aware of her surroundings... her vulnerability. How had she allowed herself to be here again, out at night – no one knowing where she was.... Her pulse pounded in her head. She turned to flee but Scott caught her arm and yanked her around. There was a hardness to his face that she had never seen before.

She struggled to get out of his grip. "Let me go!"

"You're not going anywhere," he said coolly. With a sickening feeling she realized she recognized that voice... from the night in the forest!

"What are you doing?" She tried desperately to pry his hand from her wrist. "You're hurting me!"

He grabbed her other wrist and pulled her towards him. He wrapped her in his arms and pressed her to his chest. She could feel his hot breath in her ear. She went dead still. Escape was impossible. He was holding her so tight she had trouble breathing; she was being crushed. She felt his hands moving slowly up and down her back. Then he began to stroke her hair. "You feel so good," he said quietly. He buried his face in her hair, inhaled deeply. She was too terrified to voice anything out loud, but inside her head the screaming was deafening – overwhelming to the point that it overrode her ability to think... prevented her from finding a way to save herself... never had she felt so powerless.

After a while Scott's caresses became gentler. She felt the tension leaving his arms and his hold on her lessening. She could breathe again. Then he released her and stepped back. She remained frozen, her mind whirling. He looked at her with miserable eyes. "You're free," he said. "Go! Get away from me while you still can."

Her legs sprang into action and she ran a few yards as fast as she could, but then something made her stop. She turned and glanced back. Scott was seated on a log, doubled over with his head in his hands, no longer threatening. She rubbed her wrists as she appraised the pitiable figure. Slowly, she approached and sat down beside him. "I'm still here."

He was silent for a long time, then began speaking.

"My brother has been protecting me and my mother for years," he said. "My dad's a mean son-of-a-bitch, a total loser. He claims to be a salesman but he hasn't worked in over a year. And he's a liar. When your dad came to our house that night, he had no idea whether I had been out, but he didn't let on. He covered for me because he's all about keeping what goes on in our family private. No matter what. He beat the shit out of me later though."

"Oh, Scott," she said.

"He started being mean to my mom a long time ago but it's been getting worse lately. He's on her case all the time, belittling her and making her feel real small, especially when he's been drinking. She used to be a normal mom and would do the cooking and cleaning. She read to us when we were younger and took us on walks in the woods and stuff like that... but then she started staying upstairs more and more. I don't know what came first, her staying in bed all day or him drinking too much... it's been going on for so long. Last couple of years she didn't want to do anything at all... if she made a meal it was just frying something up or opening a can."

"Was he hurting her?" asked Jane.

"They were both hurting each other, in their own ways. He was drinking more and she was making less and less effort to make things better... that gave him more ammunition to use against her. It was a downward spiral. He had probably been pushing her around for quite a while but until recently there was never anything obvious about it. Jim had a way of letting him know he was watching out for us. And Mom tried to hide it from me and Jim. If we asked, she'd say it was nothing to worry about. It was really confusing. But after he lost his job things got really bad and by last summer there was no longer any attempt to hide it. When he loses it, he slaps her across the face right in front of us. And he throws stuff… dishes, boots, whatever comes to hand and he doesn't care who sees it or who gets hurt. Jim started putting himself between them and taking the brunt of the violence. He's bigger than my dad now and could easily deck him but he never wanted to fight Dad, he only ever wanted to stop him from hurting us. If not for Jim who knows…."

His voice trailed off… then started up again. "This afternoon Mom was up in her room, and Dad had been drinking whiskey in front of the TV all day. He got hungry and went to find her. He dragged her down the stairs and threw her onto the kitchen floor, called her pathetic and ordered her to make him something to eat. I tried to help her up but he slammed me against the door jamb. He was winding up to kick her when Jim burst in… and grabbed him… tried to pin his arms down. Dad went crazy…. He's really strong when he's mad. He got out of Jim's hold and tried to punch him but Jim overpowered him and tossed him on the ground. Mom was crying and begging Dad to leave us boys out of it. When Jim turned around to help her, Dad got up from all fours and then just launched himself… Jim didn't have a chance to see him coming. I yelled but it was too late. Dad crashed into him with all his weight and Jim flew backwards and his head slammed into the corner of the countertop. The sound was sickening."

"Oh my god," said Jane.

"Jim was lying on the floor unconscious and bleeding. My mom started screaming and my dad ran out of the house. Mom went to Jim and yelled for me to call the ambulance and the police. I wanted to… but I couldn't move. I was paralyzed." He bent over and put his head in his hands again. Shudders racked his slender frame.

"It isn't your fault," she said as she placed her arm around his back.

"Jim and I have been taught never to bring people into the house. We were to stay out of view. To be unseen and left alone. They both wanted that… it was about the only thing they agreed on."

"When you never invited me to your place," Jane said, "I figured it was because you knew I didn't like Jim."

"Tonight, seeing Jim on the floor, I knew I should call for help, but I couldn't make myself do it. I panicked and ran out of the house and I didn't stop until I was deep in the woods. I was useless when Jim needed me most." He drew his sleeve across his face to wipe away the tears. "Jim acts like a bully but that's not who he is."

"Then why is he mean to everyone all the time?" she asked. "And to me? I'm not a threat."

"Think about it," said Scott. "Your dad is a cop. He doesn't want you getting close to us in case you see something and tell your parents. Jim and I are trying everything within our power to hold things together, at least until we finish school."

"I thought it was Jim who lured me into the woods. That he had figured out our code and that you were covering for him," said Jane. "Until I saw your arm all chewed up."

"He would never hurt you. In fact, he likes you a lot."

"That's hard to believe."

"Why do you think he did what he did for Helen?"

"What do you mean? What did he do for Helen?"

"He jammed Bobby into a locker until he was crying like a baby to be let out. Jim made him retract his lies about Helen."

"Jim caused Bobby to change his story? Why would he get involved?"

"Because he hates bullies. People were taking Bobby's word over Helen's. And I guess he wanted to help your family.... I have to go to him."

She reached over and took his hand. "I'm coming with you," she said. "We have two bikes in the carport. You can take Helen's and we can be at the hospital in half an hour."

"If we hurry maybe we can avoid getting caught," Scott said.

CHAPTER 31

She had only been to a hospital once before and that was to see her mother and newborn Andy. This would be nothing like that.

"Room 108." The nurse's white shoes slapped the floor officiously as she hurried back to the administration desk. She whispered to the clerk. The clerk nodded and reached for the phone.

Jane followed Scott as he strode down the corridor. The place reeked of antiseptic and urine. Fluorescent lights clung like cobwebs to the ceiling.

In the hospital room Scott flung aside the white curtain and gasped. She hesitated at the threshold, afraid of what she might see, then swallowed hard and went in. Jim's face was swollen, and both eyes were ringed with dark circles. His lips were blue and cracked. His head was wrapped in gauze bandages, a large patch of dried blood showing on his temple. The rest of his body was covered by blankets except for one arm which was connected to an IV line and an electronic monitor that beeped and whooshed steadily.

Scott took his brother's hand. "Jim... it's Scotty. I'm here. Everything is going to be okay."

There was no response.

He tried again. "Mom's okay. She's in a safe house. Dad won't be able to hurt her ever again." He peered into his brother's face. "Can you hear me? I'll go find a place for us to live, okay? Jim? Just like we planned. Remember?"

CLOMP CLOMP CLOMP.

Someone was coming down the corridor toward the room. Jane and Scott looked at each other and held their breath but the footsteps carried on down the hallway and faded away. Phew!

She put her hand on top of his. "We can't stay much longer," she whispered. "That rat-fink of a nurse has probably already told the police we're here."

Scott nodded. He leaned over his brother and kissed him gently on the forehead. He tucked in the sheets, then looked at Jane. "We can't both leave him."

She nodded. "I'll stay."

He looked at her gratefully. "Tell him I'll come for him as soon as I have a plan," he said. "I'm going to hang out at that shack we found on Mount Seymour, stay out of sight until I figure things out."

"Okay, I'll bring you food and other supplies tomorrow."

Scott walked to the end of the bed and grabbed the stack of blankets heaped at Jim's feet. Then he went to the window and opened it, ushering in a blast of cold night air. He stuck his head out and looked down to the ground. "It's only a ten-foot drop…." He threw the blankets into the darkness then looked over at Jane.

"PAGING DR. SWAN… PAGING DR. SWAN."

"Get going, or I'm in all this trouble for nothing," she said.

He crossed the room and took her hands in his. He was so close she could feel the warmth of his breath. She closed her eyes and felt him lean down until his face was next to hers. Their lips touched and rather than pulling away this time his pressed gently against hers. His mouth was soft and warm. It felt like the rest of her body had ceased to exist; her lips were the only thing that mattered. Then he gently lifted her chin, bent his head down and lightly ran his mouth down the line of fresh scar tissue on her neck. Suddenly, the rest of her body was back with her – and it was awash with sensations so powerful she could barely breathe. Pleasure yes, but an ache too, the two sensations intertwined, inseparable. Amazing! She leaned in until their bodies were pressed together, a perfect fit.

But then Scott stepped back and broke the spell. She opened her eyes. He squared her shoulders and looked at her seriously. She saw pain in his face. Were those tears? He looked like he was about to speak but couldn't.... Then the words came.

"I'm not the one you want."

"No... don't say that... let me be the judge of what's right for me," she said, as she leaned into him once more. He wrapped her in his arms and held her tight. Never had she felt such a strong bond with another person. She wanted the feeling to last forever but soon, too soon, she felt his embrace loosening. She looked into his eyes, searching for an explanation.

"Tell Jim I love him," was all he said.

Then he wiped his eyes with his sleeve and went over to the window. In one smooth motion he perched on the sill, pulled his knees to his chest, swivelled and dropped out of sight. Jane ran to the window and watched his lanky form loping away in the hazy lamplight. He never even looked back. Of course he loved his brother, but... what about her?

Jim stirred and moaned. Jane looked back at the boy in the bed. Her mind reeled at what this young man had endured both physically and emotionally. It felt she was seeing him for the first time. She understood now why he distanced himself from other kids, why he'd developed an exterior as hard as nails. It all made so much sense in hindsight. How he must have hated her and the other kids whose charmed lives were playing out all around him. No wonder he was angry.

She moved to his side. His breathing sounded stronger. He opened one eye, the other twitched but stayed glued shut.

"Scott?" he whispered.

"It's me, Jane. Scott was here but he had to leave. The authorities are after him."

She found a glass with some water on the side table and moistened his parched lips.

"I heard his voice. What happened?"

"You've been hurt and you are in the hospital."

"How bad is it?"

She didn't know what to say. She could see his mind working.

"I remember... my father..." He stopped mid-sentence. "Where's Scotty?"

"Don't worry, he's okay. They have arrested your dad and your mom is safe."

"Scotty's safe too, then?"

"Yes, he is fine. You stepped in and protected them both," she whispered. "Now you just need to get well."

He tried to speak but his voice was so faint she could barely hear. She moved closer and leaned down. "What are you trying to say?"

"Tell them to let me die," he said.

A chill ran through her. "You don't know what you're saying. You're hurting now but you'll feel better soon."

"No, I won't. It's only going to get worse for me. I'm going to end up just like him... a bully... the kind of man that hurts his own family. I'd rather die than be that man."

She took his hand. "It doesn't have to be that way. People can choose how they behave – how they treat others."

"I used to believe that, but not anymore. I see him in me, his intimidation tactics, the bullying, even the violence... they've become a part of me now. Sure, I can act normal sometimes, but when I get angry I lose control. I used to think I could manage it, that it was all just a front I was putting on, but now I'm not so sure."

She squeezed his hand. "Don't give up on yourself. I see you differently now. That's a start, right?"

"If he had kicked her, I would have killed him. That's the person I have become."

"No," she said. "You saved her and you protected Scott too – that's who you are."

There was silence for a while then he said in a stronger voice, "You know who I admire most in the neighbourhood?"

She shook her head, "Who?"

"Your dad."

Jane was dumbfounded. She had always been embarrassed by the fact that her father was so straight and uptight, never letting go and having fun at block parties like the other dads. He was a 'square,' as Helen often said.

"He's a good person. He has a proper respect for other people and the law and all that. He has a tough job but I can tell he loves it. My dad always hated his jobs and the people he had to deal with. He called the customers 'suckers' behind their backs. Then he came home and took it out on us. I started to hate him a long time ago. Then one day I noticed I was doing the same things I hated him for. Worse than that, so was Scott...."

"Scott?" said Jane, softly.

"Just early signs... but it's there. I will never forgive Dad for that. Scott is the best thing about our family... but my father was destroying him too."

There it was, the truth. She had experienced Scott's turmoil first-hand. She felt ill at the thought of him being exposed to so much abuse. How could someone so sensitive not be affected?

"Jane, I know I've treated you bad – probably worse than anyone else," said Jim. "I want you to know that I think you're really... different from other girls... free-spirited and... brave. I'm sorry for everything I did. It was me who destroyed your coffee experiment behind the curtain in the science classroom."

"That was you? We thought it was the janitor. Why would you do such a thing?"

Jim's mouth tugged down at the corners. "I don't know... to spoil something joyful maybe. I saw how much fun you and Clara were having with it... so I destroyed it." Moisture glistened in his eyes and nostrils. "I did it purely to be mean.

"I'm gonna tell it all now," he went on, his voice cracking. "I let Rosie out of your house that night you went into the woods. My parents had been arguing for weeks. Scott and I had been staying out of the house as much as possible all summer long – the tension in there was horrible. That night we were up in my room, hoping for things to settle down but then Mom came upstairs and sat at the end of my bed. She was upset but very firm. She told us that she was going to leave Dad and that she wanted us to think about whether we would go with her or stay in the house with him."

Jim coughed, spitting out some bloody saliva, then continued determinedly, "She wanted us with her but said it would mean moving and changing schools because we would be relying on government assistance. Scott got really upset. He said he didn't want to stay with Dad but he didn't want to change schools either. It was if a switch flipped in his head. He got really angry with her, blaming her for everything... saying it was her fault Dad was pissed all the time. He was even mad at your mom for giving her ideas about becoming more independent. He punched a hole in the wall, stormed into his room and locked the door. I tried to talk to him but he wouldn't answer. Eventually I managed to pry my way in – his window was open and he was gone. That really scared me. I could see he had signalled you because the magnifying lens was set up. I knew you were in danger... I'd never seen him so worked up...."

"Wait a second," she said, raising a hand. "You knew about the mirror in the tree?"

"I helped him set it up and steer the beam towards your house. He was so excited when you joined in. I was jealous and came close to destroying it many times."

"You knew about our messages?"

"Sometimes I was in his room when he was signalling with you."

"What? You were there... in his room?" She felt her pulse rate spike.

"Ya... I even helped him out once in a while."

"What do you mean... helped him out?"

"If he was having trouble thinking of something to say... like that time you said he was cool. He started to reply but didn't know how to finish... it was getting awkward... you were waiting... I said, 'Beautiful...tell her she's beautiful.'" His voice dropped off to an almost inaudible murmur... "Because it's true...."

Jane's hands flew up to her mouth and her stomach heaved. *No! No!*

Jim gathered his strength and then carried on speaking, eyes closed.

"That night, when I knocked on your door. I had no idea what I was going to say to your parents, but I knew I had to do something. Luckily it was your little brother who answered the door. Rosie was behind him and charged past us then took off like a torpedo. I've never seen a dog run like that, head down, low to the ground, taking giant strides. He must have sensed that you were in danger. I tried to follow but he vanished into the forest. I didn't know which trail to take and so I had to turn back and wait it out."

Jim took a laboured breath. "It seemed like forever, but eventually Scott climbed back in his window and everything came out... how an animal had attacked him... how you had been left in the woods. He wanted to go back but he was chewed up pretty bad. I said I'd go. I told him to clean himself up and then I ran downstairs. I was in the front hall about to leave when your dad came bursting through the front door. That's when we knew you were all right....

"I was going to take the blame, you know, cover for Scott but then I changed my mind... This was really serious, and I wanted Scott to take responsibility... you know... face some consequences. Well, my dad made sure that didn't happen." He paused, exhausted. "So now you know everything...." His voice trailed off.

She stared at the boy in the bed. He had drifted into sleep.

Jane was paralyzed. The hospital room dissolved around her and the beeps and whirrs of the medical equipment faded. The floor under her feet shifted then fell away. She felt suspended in midair for a moment, but then she was free-falling... free-falling through all the events of the last summer... All those messages... all those afternoons on the trails and on the mountain. What they had was private; a special connection forged by shared confidences. But no, none of it was real. Scott had been sharing everything with his brother. And the most intimate message, the one she had replayed in her mind at least a thousand times, wasn't even from him!

Tears welled up in her eyes. Her perception of everything she had lived through in the summer was false. Jim was the polar opposite of a bully; he was steadfast and caring, doing what he thought was best for his family. And Scott was not who she thought he was either. When he had reached out to her, she'd offered friendship and maybe something more – but what had he wanted from her? Had she been nothing more than a novelty to him, some kind of sick science experiment? In all the time they had spent together he had not revealed anything about the terrible dynamic within his family or his growing anger towards his parents. He had held everything close to his chest and shown her only the sweet side of himself. The trust he had cultivated had enabled him to lure her into the forest that night! And even afterwards, her faith in him had been so strong that seeing Rosy's bite marks had not completely convinced her that it was him that night. It had all seemed so out of character. But was it? And now he was waiting for her in a cabin on Mt. Seymour.

� ✕ ✖

"They're in here," the nurse said as she opened the door to room 108. Bud rushed to the bedside while his colleague from the night shift cased the room.

"Jane, I was so worried!" His words tumbled out.

She sprang to her feet and rushed into his arms. "Dad! I thought I was helping but…."

"The other boy's not here," said the night cop.

Bud ignored him. "Everything is going to be okay, honey. I'm here now." He held Jane against his chest and stroked her head, waiting patiently for her sobs to stop. He gently wiped the tears from her cheeks with a tissue. The way he used to do when she was small. "Do you know where Scott is?"

He looked into her eyes – saw that she couldn't speak. "It's okay, honey. Take your time."

✠ ✕ ✠

The turbulence in her head escalated to chaos as her emotions spiraled out of control. She felt herself decompensating, disintegrating into a thousand disconnected fragments. She clung to her father fearful that her legs would give way. She thought of all the signs she had misread or ignored. What was going on with her? Why hadn't she been able to see what had been right in front of her? Her analytical mind, usually her most reliable accomplice and ally, had deserted her when she needed it most! Or... had she suppressed it? Why had she not asked any questions about Scott's family when they were together? Or about his feelings? Even tonight, when the opportunity had presented itself, she had not asked him about that night in the forest; yet she had committed to helping him hide from the police! She shuddered; all her worst fears about growing up had become a sickening reality. She had been a fool, believing things because she wanted them to be true... tossing judgment out the window. And she had put herself at tremendous risk – multiple times.

Gradually she sensed her father's presence... felt his strength flowing into her... grounding her. Slowly the internal churning settled and splintered thoughts began coalescing. The room rematerialized around her and objects and people came into view. She could feel her physical strength and balance returning. Most welcome of all, she sensed her mental focus sharpening, honing in on the corrective measures needed.

She knew now what she would do. She left her dad's embrace, walked resolutely to the window and stared down at the street, to where she had last seen Scott. Then she turned to face the two officers, arms crossed, jaw set.

"The boy you're looking for jumped out this window fifteen minutes ago and is heading to a shack on Mount Seymour. I'll take you there in the morning."

CHAPTER 32

1987

The bathwater had become tepid and her wine glass was empty. There was nothing left of the candle but a small mound of warm wax. Jane could see from the hint of light coming through the small bathroom window that dawn was not far off. She reached out a hand and ran her fingertips along the familiar tract of scar tissue that started at her chin and travelled down her neck to her collarbone.

Chilled, she pulled the plug and turned on the shower. Standing under the hot spray brought her back to the problem at hand. Julian would be returning soon, best to get some rest. She towelled off and slipped on her nightie.

"Well?" came a familiar voice.

She looked toward the mirror.

Her childhood friend, now a grown woman, was sizing her up disapprovingly from the glass.

"Hello, Clara."

"It took me over a decade to come out to you," said Clara in a soft voice.

Jane was jolted back in time, to a dinner in Chinatown three years earlier. Clara had introduced her new 'friend' Rhonda and the three of them had sat at a round table next to a window with Peking duck strung like laundry along a clothesline. It had taken her half the evening to figure out what was happening – the closeness between the two of them becoming palpable. In her mind's eye she saw herself thrusting back her chair and storming out of the restaurant. It was the last time they saw each other.

"You didn't have the courage to tell me on your own," Jane said to the mirror. "You brought backup."

"I was terrified of your reaction. You had become so adamant about relationships requiring complete honesty. Transparency you called it. I found it oppressive. I knew I had left things for too long and that the evening would be painful for both of us. I brought Rhonda because I could count on her in a way I could never count on you."

Jane winced but pressed on. "I was blind-sided. Totally shocked. How could you keep something so important hidden from me for so many years? You had a whole separate life. I thought we trusted each other and shared everything. I felt betrayed. It was as if I had been pushed off a cliff backwards and was plummeting towards the rocks below. It's the worst feeling in the world. I never, ever, wanted to experience it again... and you knew it."

"I know, and I'm sorry. Those events back in high school," said Clara from her side of the mirror. "But that summer wasn't only about you. When I learned about your friendship with Scott, I was heartbroken, completely devastated. I knew you would never love me the way I loved you. And there was no one I could talk to. It was the most painful period of my life. I was just beginning to understand myself. We hung out together almost every day, but you were completely absorbed with your own stuff and didn't pay any attention to me. You were supposed to be my friend, but I'd never felt so alone."

"That's not fair, we were just kids back then."

"As were those Mason boys."

"But they misled me; they toyed with me."

"No. They reached out to you. And you cut them off at the

knees. Even after you learned about their horrendous circum-
stances, you refused to speak to either one."

She was taken aback by this unexpected criticism but
quickly reassured herself. Those boys had gotten what they
deserved. She returned her attention to the image in the mirror. "This isn't about them, is it, Clara? Like you said, it's
about you and me. You could have found a time to tell me you
were gay. We hung around together a lot at UBC and afterwards too. I would not have judged—."

"Stop! You had no right to know until I decided to tell you.
You have no right to anyone's personal story until they're
ready to share it."

"A relationship is based on trust. Your deception ended
ours."

"Nope, you ended it," said Clara. "Three years ago when
you stomped out of that restaurant without finishing your
chow mein... like all those other relationships you have ended
before they had a chance to develop. And just like the one with
Julian that you're about to end."

"What do you know about Julian?" said Jane. "You never
met him."

"I don't need to. I know you," replied Clara, as her image
started to fade.

"Wait! Clara! Don't leave." Jane raised a hand. "I heard you
were sick. I wish Rhonda had called me before the end – not
that I blame her...." Tears, held back for years, gushed from
her eyes. A moan escaped from deep within her belly and she
buried her face in the towel and sank to her knees. How could
she have been so cruel to selfless, loving Clara?

"I'm so sorry, Clara, so sorry for... abandoning you," she
sobbed. "I knew it was wrong... I was hurt... and angry... and

so... so... so... selfish.... And, oh my god... those boys... those poor boys...."

She looked up at the mirror again, but the apparition was gone. In its place, scrawled across the steam, were letters. She stood up and moved closer – watched the letters form into words. What did they say? She wiped her eyes and looked again: *Tuum Est*. The Latin phrase was familiar; it was the motto of their alma mater.

Tuum Est: It is up to you.

CHAPTER 33

Julian let himself into the apartment. For the last six months he had been spending at least two nights a week here. He removed his black overcoat and tossed it over the back of the gold brocade sofa that Jane had scored at the local thrift shop in her student days. It weighed at least two hundred pounds and bore evidence around its edges that a prior owner was a cat lover. It was still comfortable but no way was that monstrosity going to find its way to Toronto.

"It's nasty out there," he called.

No answer.

He went into the small, galley-style kitchen decked out with cream-coloured laminated counters and avocado-green appliances and set the kettle on to boil.

"Jane?" he called. "I finished my report on the king tide expected this morning. Are you still sleeping? It's nearly half-past nine!"

"I'll just be a minute," she called.

❄ ✄ ❄

She sat up in bed and ran her hands through her hair, which must be a disaster from being slept on while still wet. Her eyes were gritty and sore. Blearily, she looked at the diamond band on the table beside her. She picked it up and admired it. Beautiful. She slipped the shimmering ring onto the finger of her left hand just as Julian nudged open the bedroom door.

"One cup of tea, strong, with milk and two sugars," he announced as he set down the tray in the spot where the ring had been. "That's quite the hairdo. Care for another go round?" He started to pull up his shirt.

Jane smiled at him. "Settle down, Casanova. We need to talk."

"About what?"

"Silly. About me... about you."

He plopped down on the bed. "Okay."

She felt light-headed, almost dizzy and took a deep breath to steady herself. "Julian, you can't spring so many surprises on me, not all at once. Even if they are good surprises... I need time to adjust – a lot more than other people might – and I need to be involved at the early stages of things or it upsets me. A marriage proposal and you want us to move to Toronto, leave my work and my family – that's just too much to throw at me."

She looked into his eyes and saw the hurt and confusion. A crease formed across his forehead, but just as quickly as it appeared, it vanished.

He reached for her hand and brought it to his lips. "Aw, I'm sorry, hon. I must admit, I've been thinking about all this and planning to surprise you for weeks now. I guess I got used to it all. I didn't think about how much of a shock it would be for you. Will you forgive me?"

"I can't come with you to Toronto."

Julian pulled back.

"At least not right away."

His face brightened a little.

"I need to finish my research first."

"I kind of expected that. I figure if I go ahead to Toronto, I can get us set up," he said happily. "How long do you need?"

"A year, at least."

"That long?" The crease reappeared. "But that's a yes?"

"Well, maybe."

"Let me sweeten the deal. You can come out for conjugal visits and when we come up for air, we can pick out a new sofa!"

Jane laughed. "What girl wouldn't jump at an offer like that!"

"Sofa shopping – an oft underestimated inducement."

"One more thing. Um... I want to keep my maiden name after we're married." She looked at him with a steady gaze.

"What?"

"Well... I've already published several research papers under Jane Stewart. An academic record is crucial for advancement and for getting funding for new projects. If I change my name, I may miss some opportunities."

"But the people in your line of work will know how to find you... they're researchers, for Christ's sake!" He laughed at his own joke but she was having none of it.

"I'm serious. And it's not just about that, it's who I am. I feel like I'd be giving away part of my identity and turning away from my family if I changed my name."

Julian's grin evaporated then he stood up and walked over to the window. She hadn't planned to say any of this. Where had it come from? It had just slipped out of her mouth.

She watched him open the curtain and stand motionless with his back to her as he looked out onto the street. Her heartbeat quickened. Was he about to bolt?

Finally, he spoke, "Jane, to be honest, I'm disappointed. I always assumed that my wife would take my name... I'm from a conservative family... tradition is particularly important to us. I think we both know how my parents would react."

She was seized by guilt. She liked Sybil and Bertie. They had been very kind to her, even though she wasn't part of their Shaughnessy set. Julian was their only child, and they had invested every morsel of their beings in him. There was no doubt that they would be hurt by her rejection of their name. Why hadn't she thought about them before she blurted out her demand?

Julian turned to face her, his mouth downturned. "But conservatism can be a mechanism of oppression," he said in his announcer voice, "a constrictive force that demands adherence to questionable societal rules. I can't imagine a worse character trait for a journalist. If I can't be open-minded about something as innocuous as a surname, then I'm in the wrong business…. Don't you see, Jane? This is why I need you in my life. I've had so much handed to me… I've rarely had to decide things for myself. But you… you challenge me… you make me think critically. I may not always agree with your views, but I love that you can always defend them. It's as if that forest you were raised in inoculated you against all social conventions. You are marvellous! And more than anything in the world I want you to be happy. So, if you want to keep your name, I'll support you all the way."

She leapt to her feet and joined him at the window.

"I love you so much!" she said, throwing her arms around him and giving herself over to emotions so raw and powerful she feared she may drown. But she was not going under, she was floating. Not just floating – sailing. She was sailing – tilting into the wind, barely in control and embracing every possible outcome. How long had it been since she felt the thrill of throwing herself at life without a thought about the consequences?

He returned her embrace then picked her up and tossed her unceremoniously onto the bed. When he leaned over, she pulled him down, rolled him onto his back and straddled him. "Since I'm on a roll here...."

"Uh-oh, haven't I suffered enough at your hands today?"

"Suffer this: I prefer to order my own drinks...."

Julian covered his face with his hands.

"No hiding from me," she said as she pried his hands away and pinned them to the pillow beside his head.

HONK! HONK! HONK!

Julian's face cracked open in a mischievous grin. "Oops!"

"Oops, what???"

"You're about to find out any second now... but... uh... last weekend I asked for your dad's permission...."

"You did what???" She glanced towards the window then back at her captive.

He looked sheepish. "I'm a traditional guy... I promise to work on that...."

She was about to launch into a lecture on the paternalistic, sexist, origins of the ritual but stopped when a vision popped into her head of how absolutely tickled her dad would have been by the gesture. And her mother too. She sighed. "Alright, I'll give you a pass this time."

Then his face turned serious. "But... um... there's one more matter we need to discuss, you know, so we can start our new life together with a clean slate." His voice trailed off.

"What?" she said. She searched his face but his expression was inscrutable. "What???" A furrow formed over her brow. How bad was it going to be? She was at the point of exhaustion already....

His face lit up. "I hate martinis. They are *foul*."

Laughter filled the room.

— The End —

Epilogue

Jane completed her leukaemia research, but her department head took all the credit. She followed Julian to Toronto and obtained her PhD at the University of Toronto before being hired by the university as a full professor. She and Julian started a family a year later. They named their daughter Clara.

Julian covered the fall of the Berlin Wall and break-up of the Soviet Union for CBC television and after a few award-winning years he was made anchor of the 6 p.m. National News. (Beating out the other qualified candidates because of his good looks.)

Helen became a style influencer on TikTok at the age of 60 with a following of three trillion.

Andy became a psychologist specializing in family counselling.

Doreen negotiated bulk purchases of Skin So Soft (spiked with DEET) for the police forces of Greater Vancouver, Northern BC, Alberta and Yukon and was later hired by Avon as a product development consultant after suggesting a line of innovative products, including compounds with SPF, essences of medicinal plants and a full range of skin products for men.

Bud became station captain and hired the first women officers in North Vancouver.

Scott and Jim lived with teacher Arthur Klassen until they finished high school. Scott became a lighting roadie known for explosive laser shows. Jim became a police officer.

Margaret divorced George, took a cooking course, and became a cordon bleu chef.

After his divorce, George attended AA, married a Baptist missionary and moved to Uganda.

Sophie and Rosie lived long, happy lives.

ACKNOWLEDGMENTS

Thank you to Michael Kenyon, our editor, who honed our prose in subtle but crucial ways and helped us deliver a story we are ready to share. Thank you also to John Stevens for his beta reading several years ago which kept the work moving forward when we were close to abandoning it. Thank you as well to Jane Rogerson, Jim Henshall, Michael Armstrong and Donna Mooney for providing thoughtful suggestions on the manuscript which allowed us to make critical adjustments before sending it to "print." We also wish to express our appreciation for the assistance of Randy Tkatch who provided advice on the physics described in the story, the Armstrong family for hosting our Whistler Mountain writing weekend and the Bell family for hosting our Bowen Island retreat. Lastly, we wish to acknowledge the contribution of Bruce Batchelor and Agio Publishing House for seeing the book into print.

ABOUT THIS NOVEL

This novel is the collaborative work of the Vancouver-based BWB Book Club (Babes With Books). The club formed in 1999 and we have enjoyed hundreds of books and thoughtful discussions since then. At one meeting in 2010 someone said we should try authoring our own book. How hard could it be? We were all dedicated readers and writing was an important part of many of the careers we'd forged for ourselves.

Organizational meetings followed and we decided that, for the story to be authentic, writers should draw upon personal experience. Since everyone in the group was born in the 1950s to middle-class parents and most grew up in the Vancouver area, many on the North Shore, we shared common ground. We decided to write the coming-of-age story of a 12-year-old girl living with her family on the foothills of Mount Seymour.

The names of the main characters, the profession of the father and other foundational elements were drawn from suggestions thrown into a hat. Frivolous elements were randomly agreed upon before the work began. For example, the story had to include a pair of twins and the word 'iguana' had to be incorporated. From the beginning this project was meant to be fun and not taken too seriously.

The personality and appearance of Jane was the product of group discussion, as was the main plot. Other characters, like her sister, Helen, and her mother, Doreen, were developed largely by the writers responsible for the chapters in which these characters were featured.

After a few months, initial enthusiasm for the project waned and little headway was made. To reboot the project, we decided to hold a couple of weekend retreats to focus on writing. Those two weekends, on Whistler Mountain (2012) and Bowen Island (2013), resulted in great progress. At the end of every writing day, we sat down to a fabulous dinner and lots of wine. Each of us stood up and read aloud our contribution to the story. Of course, the new works introduced unexpected twists and turns. The uproarious laughter we shared was all the reward we needed to press on. However, because everyone had been writing simultaneously as opposed to serially, the work contained many inconsistencies in the story lines, along with a variety of writing styles. This created challenges but also opportunities for individual voices to be heard.

At one of our subsequent regular book club meetings, we assigned ourselves the task of describing Jane's sexual awakening. Each would write the chapter and we would draw upon the best versions for our book. We all dutifully reported in at the next meeting and, after copious amounts of red wine, read aloud our proposed contributions. Again, we laughed until our stomachs ached.

The editing process stalled for years as we all became busy with work and family lives. Then COVID-19 came along freeing up a lot of time. The manuscript was dusted off and the work of stitching it together re-commenced. By December 2023 we were ready to say enough is enough: this was never going to be perfect, no matter how much time we spent ironing out lumps and bumps. We decided to complete the editing work by the end of 2024 to mark the 25th anniversary of the book club.

As primary editor, I was tasked with melding together the various parts of the story and synchronizing ideas, perspectives, and narrative strategies. I added several connective passages and a couple of short chapters to make the work more cohesive. Where necessary, I tweaked storylines, but

At left, waving: Maureen Richardson. Back row: Deb Tivy, Lea Tkatch, Joanne Webster, Cathy Kershaw, Eleanor Wright and Lynda Stevenson. Lounging on the log: Judy Rothwell and Linda Stevens. Playing in the sand in front: Sue Johnson.

otherwise tried to preserve everyone's writing style, ideas and imagery. The final product is a patchwork, born of ten separate keyboards and the reader may be reminded of this as she experiences changes in tone throughout the work. While everyone participated in the writing of the story, contributions varied with some members producing more of the written text and others working more on the editing and publishing phases of the project. In the end, every one of us can say: *"We* did it!"

What have we produced? A story written for no other reason than the joy of working together to create something unique. What do we hope for? That our tale entertains, that our girl Jane and her family members are relatable and that each of our individual voices can be heard. And if our bold attempt to write a novel inspires your book club to pursue something similar, we would love to hear from you. Contact us at *bwbook25@gmail.com*. For more of the backstory behind this project, visit our website: *beyondreflection-novel.ca*

— Linda Stevens *on behalf of the BWB contributors:*

Sue Johnson, Cathy Kershaw, Maureen Richardson, Judy Rothwell, Linda Stevens, Lynda Stevenson, Deb Tivy, Lea Tkatch, Joanne Webster and Eleanor Wright.

ABOUT THE AUTHORS

SUE JOHNSON

Sue was born on Vancouver Island and later moved to the North Shore. Growing up close to the mountains she became an enthusiastic skier and continues to enjoy the great outdoors. After high school she attended university, then college, and then worked downtown in the corporate world. She got the bug for residential real estate and built a successful career spanning more than 37 years. She is married and the proud mother of two daughters and grandmother to two beautiful granddaughters. Her passions are tennis, travel and learning an elusive game called golf. Her quest in life is to have more grandchildren than Linda. Sue worked on the chapters involving Helen and was primary writer of the scenes involving Miss Twist, Candy Wright, and the Spring Fling dance. She also contributed hours to the editing process.

CATHY KERSHAW

Cathy was born and raised in Vancouver. She studied education at UBC with a major in Physical Education (B.Ed.) and later studied marketing and sales at BCIT. She worked with major consumer packaging and pharmaceutical companies as a sales representative. Now retired, she is an avid reader and plays tennis and golf. Cathy credits her membership in the book club with fostering strong, long-lasting friendships and introducing her to books she may never have otherwise read. Among other contributions Cathy collaborated with Linda on the Lions Gate Hospital scenes and participated in progress reviews.

MAUREEN RICHARDSON

Maureen was born and raised in Vancouver. After high school she lived in Italy for a year, then obtained a B.A. from UBC. She worked in a television newsroom for 35 years as a control room director and is now retired. She is an avid tennis player and cyclist, and a hobby photographer. But her great passion is travel and she is currently on a quest to travel to a hundred countries. Maureen took the group photo on page 203 and contributed to the writing in several foundational sections including the scene featuring grown-up Jane at the Stanley Park Teahouse and the scenes where young Jane becomes intrigued by the flashing lights. She was also a major participant in the editing process.

JUDY ROTHWELL

Judy was born in North Vancouver at Lions Gate Hospital. She graduated Delbrook High School, took a year sabbatical traveling in Europe, completed studies at Simon Fraser University then became a professional accountant working for a major firm. She has a daughter and a grandson. Happily married, she's now living on the Sunshine Coast. She performs extensive volunteer work with a variety of charities and is especially dedicated to mission work in Africa. "It's been a great joy to spend time in Vancouver with the BWB girls amidst the laughter, sharing stories and views on the latest novel!" Judy, along with Sue and Deb, created the storyline featuring Helen.

LINDA STEVENS

Linda grew up in North Vancouver then attended UBC where she obtained a B.A. (theatre) and LLB. She practiced law for 25 years then retired to focus on her tennis game and other neglected interests, including her husband, three children and seven grandchildren. When not hosting social gatherings, she loves exploring deserts and making pickles and jams during summers spent in the South Okanagan. Linda developed the main plot involving young Jane and provided the impetus that kept the project moving forward.

LYNDA STEVENSON

Lynda was born in Greece, lived in Australia, and then moved to Canada. She was employed by 3M for 15 years as a systems specialist. She married and started a family and simultaneously founded a national telecommunications distribution company which she and her husband operated for 25 years across Canada and the USA. She is retired and having fun reading, baking, hiking, gardening, playing pickleball and tennis. She enjoys great friendships, and her grandchildren continuously bring joy and keep her young at heart. Lynda, together with Sue, created the character of Doreen and the sub-plot related to her Avon ambitions.

DEB TIVY

Deb grew up in North Vancouver and ventured over to the west side to UBC where she graduated with a science degree. She is a CPA and enjoyed a career in finance and human resource management in the airline, technology and insurance industries. In retirement Deb dabbles in art and photography. Deb is the official leader of the BWB book club and is to be credited with keeping our membership active and connected over the last 25 years. She wrote the camping trip chapter, Ambleside family picnic scene and collaborated on the scenes involving Helen. She was also involved in the editing process and created the painting for the back cover.

LEA TKATCH

Lea was born in Vancouver and raised merely steps from Kitsilano's beachfront where she grew to love and respect the ocean. At age fifteen she ran away from home, lived on a farm in Richmond where she boarded her horse, and worked full time after school and on weekends pumping ice cream and flipping burgers in Steveston until graduation. After a short stint in fashion retail, Lea turned her organizational superpower to administration and spent the next 40 years in the high-tech sector providing executive support, event, project and financial management services and running her own personnel placement business. After retiring in 2016, Lea began volunteering for the Vancouver Orphan Kitten Rescue Association (VOKRA), originally as a foster, then moving on to serve on the board and for eight years as finance manager.

Lea's ideas for Jane's sexual awakening scene were adopted by the group and she wrote the first draft of the scene at the base of the oak tree describing the attraction between Jane and Scott. She was part of the final review and editing.

JOANNE WEBSTER

Joanne was born in Newfoundland, grew up in Montreal and went to Queen's University where she studied history and psychology. She moved to British Columbia to become Director of Sales and Marketing for the Whistler Resort Association, leading to a 30-year career in hotel management and tourism. She is the mother of three, a proud grandmother and an avid golfer, skier, tennis player, and outdoor enthusiast. She was involved in writing the science fair chapters and helped with the final review and editing process.

ELEANOR WRIGHT

Eleanor is from Bayfield, Ontario. With a degree in nursing, she worked on a surgical ward at Women's College Hospital in Toronto then became interested in pharmaceuticals and began working in sales for Eli Lilly Canada. She was transferred to Vancouver to cover BC and Alberta and later set up her own contract sales business. "Reading is a pleasure; Travel is a passion," she says. She and her husband travel yearly, exploring the globe. Eleanor wrote nuanced descriptive passages that appear throughout the novel as well as a version of Jane's sexual awakening that had us laughing to the point of tears. Eleanor also worked on the final review and editing process.

www.ingramcontent.com/pod-product-compliance
Lightning Source LLC
Chambersburg PA
CBHW041755180626
46815CB00018B/303